It's In The Ink

Jo Lauer

DEDICATION

To all who think, live, and play outside the box.

ACKNOWLEDGMENTS

Thank you to Robbi Sommers Bryant, editor extraordinaire, who spit-shined my manuscript and turned it into this book; Joan Etchandy for research on sailing the seas; L. A. Paul for capturing the moment for my head shot; Michelle Fairbanks, for her artistic eye and cover design; and to my sister, Sue Spight, beta reader, cheerleader, and general muse.

It's in The Ink

A Little Old Ladies Mystery

Chapter One

"Fire!" yelled Amanda. She frantically fanned her hands as smoke billowed out of the ancient toaster.

Marion grabbed a tea towel, yanked the plug from the socket, and smacked the flames from the burning toast. Crumbs scattered across the counter. "Get ahold of yourself," she admonished as she gathered toast fragments and dumped them in the wastebasket.

"I guess we'll forego the toast," Amanda said. "We could do bagels under the broiler."

"No," Marion said. "Enough adventure already."

Marion Knox and Amanda Pritchard, as unlikely a pair as peanut butter and pickles, begrudgingly shared Amanda's funky brown-shingled cottage at the back of a wildly overgrown lot.

Marion's apartment building, now covered up for fumigation, had been a haven for roaches, silverfish, deadly brown spiders, and a host of other unacceptable encroachers. Amanda had been generous enough to offer a place for Marion to stay during the extermination process.

The two had become friends when they teamed up to solve some cases from the police cold files a few years earlier.

Marion had the gift of "seeing" things others couldn't detect and the ability to "stop time" to observe details that would otherwise have been missed.

Amanda, whose tenacity and odd-duck personality gained her a certain notoriety and access to otherwise unavailable resources, had been an investigative journalist covering the police beat,

"Aren't the landlords compelled to pay for a motel or something if their property becomes unlivable?" Amanda shuffled her bulk around Marion to get to the stove. She turned on the pilot under the kettle and grabbed two mugs from the cupboard.

"They are," Marion replied, "but the motel they chose is a fleabag dive down on the Avenue where hookers, junkies, and drug dealers reside." She squeezed past Amanda, took a baggie of chrysanthemum tea from the shelf, and plunked two blossoms into each cup.

"I've been thinking. Now that we're retired from the psychic sleuthing business, we should find something to do so our minds won't go to mush," Marion said.

Their last case had taken a mental and physical toll on them both.

Marion grabbed a catalog off the table and thumbed to a previously marked page. "I found a class on watercolors." She handed the pamphlet to

Amanda. "I've always wanted to paint. It's all the rage with the retirement crowd. We can take it for free, being old and all." She wrinkled her nose at the word 'old.'

Amanda poured hot water into their mugs, shooed the calico cat from her sunning spot, and settled next to Marion at the Formica kitchen table.

Amanda, an aging lesbian who had not lost her sparkle, talked up the alcohol inks class instead. *After all*, she secretly thought, *what's not to like about the sexy art teacher pictured in the pamphlet*. Amanda read the name under the photo. *Instructor*, *Jeri Kay*, *looked like a dyke*. "Who wants to do what everyone else is doing?"

"Alcohol inks? You paint and drink wine?" Marion asked. "Doesn't sound like they could do that at the JC—at least not for credit."

"No, it's *nothing* like that. Look at this YouTube tutorial. Mandy—you know, that redhead from the Peace and Justice Center—mentioned it yesterday."

Amanda shifted to the other side of the table in front of her laptop, motioned Marion to join her, and typed, "YouTube, Alcohol Ink," into the search bar.

"Will you look at that," Marion said, her eyes wide. "The way those paints blend and move around on the paper—it's like magic."

Amanda reached for the catalog and tapped on the course description. "We've *got* to learn how to do that."

"They just dropped some rubbing alcohol onto the ink. Seems like something we could teach ourselves, don't you think?" Marion said.

"Absolutely not!" Amanda replied. Her eyes shimmered mischievously. "We definitely need a professional to guide us. Someone who knows the local art scene—for supplies and all."

"Jeri Kay, in other words," Marion said. She shook her head.

"You bet." A Cheshire grin spread across Amanda's face.

Marion took the pamphlet back. "Odd name, Jeri Kay. Is Kay her last name, do you think? Or is it like "Mary Ann," but with no last name? Like Cher?" She studied the picture.

"I'm pretty sure Kay is her last name."

"Well, I'm going to call her Jeri Kay," Marion said with finality as she plunked the brochure down on the table.

"Fine," Amanda said with a shrug.

Chapter Two

Having followed a campus map to the correct room, Amanda and Marion found chairs next to each other and prepared themselves for their first class in alcohol inks.

"You look kinda cute in your apron," Marion teased.

Amanda did an exaggerated bow, pulled out their chairs, and they both sat down. Ready to paint, they pulled on blue latex gloves, tied their aprons, and waited patiently.

Lined up in front of each pair of painters were sheets of non-porous paper, a selection of twelve tiny bottles of colored inks, an array of paintbrushes, sponges, and straws. Everything had been set on top of a large plastic tablecloth covered with layers of newspaper.

"I feel like a '40s housewife ready to baste a turkey," Amanda said, looking down at her floral apron.

"Once upon a time, you *were* a '40s housewife," Marion said.

General chatter and nervous laughter came from the students, mostly middle-aged women, until the instructor, Jeri Kay, sauntered into the room.

Cut at a razor-sharp angle, Jeri's silver hair emphasized her lavender eyes. Her chiseled face with a prominent nose and squared chin brought an exotic edge to her face. She wore painters' pants and a halter-top, which showed off her tanned and toned body.

It took only one glance at Jeri for Amanda to fall into fantasies: she and Jeri Kay sailing on a summer day. Stopped at the top of a Ferris wheel. Dancing at a club.

"Good morning. I'm Jeri Kay," she said. Her voice, deep and commanding, drew in Amanda even more. As Jeri made eye contact with each student in a slow visual sweep around the table, her gaze lingered for a moment on Amanda. "I'm glad to see so many of you interested in alcohol inks."

Perspiration broke out on Amanda's forehead. Her thoughts ran amok. *Oh my God, she sees me. She can read my eyes. She knows I know. It's that gaydar thing.*

Marion glanced sideways, cleared her throat quietly, and surreptitiously hand-gestured to Amanda to close her mouth.

Amanda caught the signal. *Dear God, I must look like an idiot with my mouth hanging opened and eyes wide as baseballs.* She smacked her lips together. A silly grin crossed her face through the remaining introduction and demonstration of the inks.

When it was time for the students to apply the ink to the paper and practice the techniques, Marion nudged Amada with her elbow.

"Really? Is this what it's going to be like for the next six weeks?"

Amanda blinked as if coming out of an enchanted fog.

On the far end of fifty, Amanda was as short and solid as a tree stump. Her gray hair sported a variety of rainbow-colored stripes. Wearing one of her favorite tent dresses, leggings, and Birkenstocks, Amanda appeared unaware that she may not be a perfect match for the modelesque teacher.

"Poor dear," Marion muttered to herself, although Amanda heard.

Poor dear *what*?" Amanda replied. "I'm not—"

"Similar to cloud-gazing." Jeri Kay's words interrupted Amanda's retort. "Inks have a way of revealing secret pictures, almost like a Rorschach inkblot," Jeri said.

The students were bent over their papers, except for Amanda who looked up with rapt attention.

"Those of you with active imaginations should like that part." Again, she glanced directly at Amanda and smiled.

Amanda felt the heat as her face flushed.

After an hour of playing with the ink, class ended with a list of supplies needed before the next class. Their homework was to study their paintings.

Amanda lingered at the table as she waited for the crowd of students around Jeri to thin out. It didn't.

Marion tugged at her elbow. "There will be other opportunities. Let's swing by the art store on our way home."

As soon as they arrived home, Amanda dumped the contents of their art purchases on the kitchen table and set things up much the way they'd been in class.

"Maybe we should have lunch before we start," Marion suggested. "You know how you get when your blood sugar drops." She made a deranged face and fluttered her hands near her ears.

While Marion made tuna sandwiches and poured lemonade, Amanda scooted things back farther on the table leaving enough room to set their plates. She leaned both their class projects up against the glasses so they could study them over lunch.

"Holy Mother of God," Amanda said. "Will you look at that!" She pointed to the upper right corner of Marion's painting. "It's that woman—"

"What?" Marion squinted and leaned forward.

"Right there." Amanda outlined the area with her finger. "Isn't that the face of the old woman in yesterday's newspaper?"

"Who?" Marion's voice was even.

"You know, the one who's gone missing."

"Here, have a bite of protein." Marion handed Amanda the sandwich. "You'll feel better in a moment."

Amanda dropped her sandwich on her plate, pushed her chair back from the table, and retrieved a newspaper from a stack by the door. She opened it and pointed at the photograph.

"Listen to this," Amanda said and then began to read. "'My mother is missing,' the daughter had told reporters when she went to visit her mother in Pine Hollow Care Center last week. An APB has been put out for Esther Hart, 85-year-old female, who may have wandered away from the Center." Amanda scanned the article. "Not just any elderly woman." She looked directly at Marion then pointed to the face that had emerged from the blend of inks in Marion's painting. "*This* woman."

"No," Marion protested, yet she couldn't deny the obvious. The face in the black and white photo was the same as the face that emerged in blues and greens from her art project.

"How did you do that?" Amanda asked.

"*I* didn't do it; the ink did," Marion said, her voice defensive.

"The article goes on to say the facility closed due to bankruptcy, and the patients were transferred," Amanda said with a shake of her head. "Doesn't give a reason. Smells fishy to me."

"Those poor patients uprooted like that." Marion sighed.

"Getting old sucks."

"Well, crap!" Marion sat back in her chair, shoulders slumped. "What do we do now? We're retired, remember?"

"We can't just ignore it," Amanda said.

Sandwiches forgotten, they pulled the painting toward themselves for a closer look. As if by instinct rather than intent, Marion took a small vial of isopropyl alcohol and applied a drop directly over the face.

"No!" Amanda hollered as the face blurred, shifted, and changed. "You're destroying evidence."

"Help!" came a desperate cry from the paper before the blues and greens ran toward the center and mixed with the yellows and oranges of the painting. Marion gasped and threw her hand over her racing heart. Her jaw went slack.

"*What*?" Amanda said. Alarm rearranged her face as she stared at Marion.

"Didn't you hear that voice?" Marion said.

Amanda shook her head.

"Well, then, never mind." Marion pushed the painting away, stood, and left the room.

"You know she came to you for a reason," Amanda said a couple hours later. "We can't just ignore her."

"Coincidence, serendipity, imagination—whatever," Marion replied. "She didn't *come* to me. It was just a freakish ink accident," she said, belying what she knew to be the truth. The spirit of the elderly woman had indeed reached out to her for help. *Why do the dead always seek me out to clean up their messes*?

Frustrated with the whole discussion, Marion set her project paper in front of her and splashed it with more alcohol obliterating any dripping remains of an old, lost, or possibly dead woman. The run of orange and yellow ink created another face—a younger woman, anger in her eyes, tension in her jaw. A dark aura of gray surrounded the face.

"Oh, hell," Marion muttered. She turned away.

Amanda jumped out of her chair and leaned over Marion's painting. "There! You see? Holy Mother. The plot thickens. Who do you suppose this is?"

"Not only do I not know, but I also do not care," Marion said. *I didn't sign up for all this drama. I just wanted to learn how to paint.* She pushed her paper aside, left the table, and clicked on the TV. "*Golden Girls,*" she said.

And that was that.

Later that evening, in the privacy of her room, Amanda stared at her reflection in the mirror. "You're not getting any younger chickee," she said. It had been years since she'd had a love interest in her life. *Carpe diem*, and all that," she said as she opened her cell phone and dialed. She paced in a circle as she listened to three rings before a voice said, "This is Jeri."

"Jeri, it's Amanda Prichard—from the alcohol inks class," she managed around a lump in her throat. "Your number was on the list of supplies for class. I hope it's okay to call." She ran a knuckle across her sweaty lip.

"Amanda!" Jeri's voice was like liquid velvet.

Amanda wanted to swim in it, roll around in it, swallow it.

"So good to hear from you. I *always* want to be *available* to my students."

Amanda wondered just *how* available Jeri was. "Is it possible," Amanda swallowed hard. "I mean . . . could we meet for coffee? There's something I'd like to talk to you about—you know, about alcohol inks."

Chapter Three

Only a sliver of moonlight filtered through the window. Marion glanced at the clock. 3:00 a.m. She slid her feet into her slippers, put on her robe, grabbed her purse, and snuck out of the house. Moving robotically to her silver Honda Accord parked under the old oak tree, she got in the car and started the motor.

Marion eased down the makeshift driveway and onto the street. Once out of the neighborhood, she turned right onto the highway and took the second exit. After four blocks, she turned to follow a long driveway that ended in a deserted patch of tarmac. She put her car in park and sat idling in the still night until the call of an owl broke the spell.

"What? Where . . ." Marion's focus shifted to the white marble plaque affixed to the side of the converted mansion in front of her. Pine Hollow Care Center.

Not wanting to be conspicuous in the empty darkness, she fumbled in her purse for her cell phone instead of turning on the overhead light. She dialed and listened to the ring before a groggy-sounding Amanda answered.

"Marion? Why are you calling? Are you okay?" the words slurred together.

"I know. Sorry," Marion mumbled. "I'm not at home." She scanned the grounds through squinted eyes. The moon cast a ghostly filtered light, which did little to illuminate anything other than the treetops.

"I'm at Pine Hollow Care Center."

"What?" Amanda sounded more alert. "Why are you there?"

"I don't know exactly. I think I sleep-drove—if there is such a thing. I'm scared." A branch snapped nearby. Marion gasped and slunk down lower in the driver's seat. "It's creepy here. This place has weird energy. Like a graveyard. Can you come?" Her voice was hesitant.

"You make such a compelling argument." Amanda's voice dripped sarcasm. She yawned loudly. "Let me put some clothes on. I'll be right there."

"Hurry, okay?" Marion said.

"Yeah, yeah." Amanda hung up.

A cold sensation slithered up Marion's spine. She thought back to the last time she attended a burial. Dozens of spirits who roamed the grounds were only visible to her. They found her. They always found her. Again, the chill.

She cracked the window for some air, then immediately cranked it back. *Ectoplasm can slip through small openings.* She scanned the grounds. *Why am I thinking about ghosts?* The image of the elderly woman from her painting dropped into her mind as well as that distinct, though silent, cry for help.

"Oh, dear," Marion muttered. "This means the old woman is dead, and we have another murder on our hands." She remembered the uncanny way dead people sought her out—the dead child who'd been abducted by the local minister, the woman thrown off the balcony. They had needed her help.

She startled as headlights appeared in the driveway behind her. Amanda's car slowed to a stop as she pulled next to Marion. Amanda got out and slammed the door. Marion's shoulders jerked in response.

"Shhh," Marion warned as she climbed from her car, tightened her robe against the morning chill, and stood next to Amanda.

"So why are we here? And why are we whispering?" Amanda said. "This place looks deserted. Remember? The paper said they went bankrupt, transferred all the residents, and closed up shop," she said in her normal voice. "Well, transferred all of them except for the old lady who went missing . . . showed up in your painting."

"I'm not sure," Marion said. "I think we're supposed to look around or something."

"Do you always break and enter in your jammies and robe?" Amanda gestured to her outfit.

"This is my first B 'n E. I didn't know there was a dress code," Marion said.

"Door's probably locked, and I imagine there's an alarm system," Amanda offered.

"If they went bankrupt, maybe they didn't pay their security bill," Marion said. "Let's take a look." She flipped open her cell phone, and they followed the dim light up the path to the porch. She noticed the battery level dropping on her phone. *When was the last time she'd charged it*?

At the bottom step, Marion grabbed Amanda's elbow. "What if we get caught?" she said.

"Then you'll wish you had changed clothes," Amanda said. "Come on. Let's get this over with." She led Marion up the steps.

At the top step, they froze at the screech of a nighthawk overhead. "Maybe it's a warning," Marion said.

"Only to mice and rabbits." Amanda crossed the porch and jiggled the door handle. "Locked tight," she muttered. "Follow me."

They tried the front window and then proceeded around to the side.

"Will you look at that," Amanda said. "I'd call it divine intervention." She pointed to the glass shards on the ground from a window that had been smashed by a falling tree limb. "What are the chances, huh?" She snapped a branch from the limb, used it as a makeshift broom, and swept away the larger chunks of glass.

Several jagged pieces still protruded from the window frame. Amanda knocked them free with the branch.

"Quite the Girl Scout," Marion said. "Now what?"

"Now I hoist you through the window, and you go unlock the front door," Amanda said. "Geez, don't you read mystery novels?"

Marion shook her head.

"Watch out for the glass," Amanda ordered. "You don't have real shoes on."

Marion looked down at her slippered feet and sighed.

"Okay, I'm going to squat down. You climb on my shoulders. I'll stand up, and you can crawl in through the window," Amanda said.

"Oh, I'm not sure—"

"C'mon, c'mon. We don't want to be here when the sun rises." Amanda squatted beneath the window, and reluctantly, Marion straddled her shoulders.

"Here we go. One, two, three . . ." Amanda groaned with the strain and farted. There was no upward movement.

"Alright, that's not going to work," she said. Marion climbed off and leaned against the building.

"Now what?"

Amanda bent her knees and said, "Give me your foot."

Marion put her foot in Amanda's cupped hands.

"Ready?" Amanda said.

"No." Marion inhaled and imagined herself light as a cloud. "Okay. Now."

Amanda heaved upward once again, panting with the effort.

Marion clawed her hands along the wall.

"Just a little higher," she called over her shoulder.

"Fuck," Amanda sputtered.

"Got it," Marion said as she clamored through the window.

She landed with a *thud* and surveyed the room. "This must be a storeroom," she called back to Amanda. "Nothing but shelves, boxes, brooms, mops, and stuff."

Just then, her cell phone battery died, and the room went black. A small creature with sharp toenails ran over the top of her slipper. "Dear God," she screamed.

Within seconds, Marion heard Amanda yell and imagined some night watchman, psycho neighborhood creeper, or maybe the police had jumped Amanda in the dark. She shuffled back to the window and leaned out. "*Amandaaa*," she called frantically.

"I'm okay," Amanda called. "Just twisted my ankle. You okay? Why were you yelling?"

"My phone died. I have no light. I don't know where I am. And I think a rat ran over my foot," Marion said. She leaned out of the window as far as she could. "Where are *you*? Do you need help?"

"Around front," Amanda said. "I took off my sock and am using it to wrap my ankle. You're going to have to find the front door and come get me."

"Why can't I just crawl back out the window?" Marion said. "It's too dark in here."

"We need to unlock the door," Amanda said, her voice strained.

Inside the house, Marion felt her way along the wall. She stomped her slippered feet with each step to deter a rodent attack. Working her way around an outcropping of shelving, she knocked a box onto the floor. The contents, apparently metal bedpans, clattered.

"What are you *doing* in there?" Amanda called from a distance.

Marion took a ragged breath and tried not to cry. *It's just an old house*, she told herself as she inched along. Her hand finally found the doorknob. She froze. *What if it's locked?* She felt her heart tighten as she seized the knob, turned it, and gave it a mighty shove. The door swung open. There was just enough diffused light coming through the windows for Marion to orient herself. She could see a long hallway ending in a large open room.

She stood for a moment, regulating her breathing and gathering her courage, then worked her way along the wall. Her hand fumbled onto a light switch. *As if that's going to do me any good*, she thought. Just for the hell of it, she flipped the switch. The hallway flooded with light. "Oh, my God," she said and laughed with relief.

Hurrying through the large room toward the front door, she unlocked the deadbolt, stepped out onto the porch, and ran down the steps.

Amanda sat on the ground in a small pool of light from the window above. "I think I sprained my ankle," she complained.

"We should get you to the hospital." Marion helped Amanda to a standing position.

"The house is unlocked, the lights work, and it's still dark outside. I say we look through the house while we can," Amanda said.

"Don't be ridiculous," Marion said.

Even so, Amanda leaned heavily on the railing and hopped on her good foot all the way up the steps. She stopped on the porch to wipe her sweaty brow. "So, ah . . . what, exactly, are we looking for?" she said.

"Clues?" Marion replied as she followed Amanda to the porch. "I'll know it when I see . . ." She stood statue still, her eyes glazed over.

"Marion? Marion, what is it? Don't you be having a stroke on me now." Amanda's voice was tight with worry.

Marion turned, and as if in a trance, glided down the hallway.

"Hey! Wait up. Don't leave me here," Amanda called, hopping on her good foot.

Amanda hopped into a bedroom lined with metal cots, six on each side. Some had bare mattresses, some soiled linen. The odor of urine and bleach hung like a dirty sheet. She felt drawn to a bed at the far end of the room. She approached, scanned the bed and rumpled sheet, then focused on a small corner of paper protruding from underneath the mattress. She bent down, pulled the paper free, and read, *Help me. I'm next*, printed in ink.

Below, was a list of dates and a brief description of abuses perpetrated on the bedridden patients by the staff: *August 13, Millie—scratched staff—fingernails cut to quick and bleeding*; *August 15, Mack— wouldn't eat—hit with spoon, knuckle broken.*

"Check this out," Amanda said as Marion came into the room behind her. "A list of abuses . . ."

The list ended with *August 20, Annabelle—wet the bed overnight—left on bedpan all day, bedsore infected.* A sickening list of "crimes" and "punishments," enough for an ombudsman to inspect and shut down the facility. At the top right-hand corner in small script were the letters "cc."

"Looks like she wanted to make sure whoever found this knew it wasn't the only copy. Someone may have found the original," Amanda said to Marion who was now at Amanda's side.

"If it was the wrong person, Esther could be in serious trouble," Marion replied.

"Let's get out of here. I have some computer research to do." Amanda leaned on Marion and hop-shuffled her way back to their cars.

"You can't drive," Marion said, stating the obvious. "We'll have to leave your car here overnight. I'll ask someone from painting class to drive us back after class."

Amanda cast a tentative look at her faded-blue VW Bug. "I guess it will be safe enough here, the place being deserted and all," she agreed. "Let's drive back through town and stop at the all-night diner for pancakes."

"I don't know . . . I think I've had all the excitement I can handle for one night," Marion said.

"You find pancakes too exciting?" Amanda furrowed her eyebrows.

Marion turned her blinkers on and headed toward town.

Chapter Four

After pancakes and coffee, neither woman felt like returning to bed. They detoured to the hospital where Amanda's ankle was x-rayed. "Not broken or sprained, just severely twisted," she was told. "Elevate and ice it."

Sure, okay, Amanda thought. *At least I can do a computer search on the Pine Hollow Care Center.*

Just then a loud knock banged on the front door. "Marion, can you get that?" The doorbell rang again. "Darn, where is she?" Amanda wobbled into the hall where she heard Marion singing in the shower.

"Good God, I'm coming," Amanda shouted. "Don't break the door down." She limped to the door and opened it to two surly looking police officers. She squinted more to clear her mind than her eyesight.

"Amanda Pritchard?" the taller of the two officers said.

She nodded.

"Come with us, please."

"What? No . . . I've got work to do," Amanda said. "What's this about?"

"You're under arrest for breaking and entering the Pine Hollow Care Center. We found your car in their parking lot this morning. There was a broken window, the door was unlocked, and the lights left on."

"I can explain—" Amanda began.

"I'm sure you can," The officer cut her off mid-sentence. "Down at the station." He read her the Miranda Rights. "Get your purse. Let's go."

"I need to tell my—"

"Now." The officer turned her toward the door.

In a daze, she grabbed her coat and purse and hobbled out the door.

Refreshed from a long, hot shower, Marion stepped out of the bathroom.

"Your turn," she called to Amanda. Hearing no response, Marion went into the living room. The computer screen was on, and the Google search page awaited further instruction, but no Amanda.

"Huh?" Marion said. "Amanda?" she called as she walked into the kitchen. Nothing. She opened the back door, glanced around the garden, and startled a deer nibbling on a lettuce plant. No Amanda.

"Well," Marion said with exasperation. "It's as if she's been spirited away." She backtracked through the house and noticed Amanda's purse and coat were gone. She stepped into the front yard and scanned the overgrowth. Not a sign of her roommate anywhere. Marion's car was just where she'd left it.

"I don't know what to do," she said to a woodpecker as it tapped away on the oak tree in the corner of the yard. The bird offered no suggestions. "I've never had to deal with anything like this before." Scowling in confusion, she went back inside and sat on the couch.

"Ah," she said, smacking her head. She dialed Amanda's cell and was directed to leave a message. She threw her cell phone on the couch.

Down at the local police station, Amanda gave a rundown of her 3:00 a.m. escapade to Detective Clyde Barrell. This being a small town, the detective remembered Marion's name from the previous year— she'd called in two false alarms based on her 'psychic abilities.' They'd referred her to County Mental Health for evaluation.

It appeared Amanda was also a bit of a crackpot, talking about faces of missing people appearing in paintings and cryptic notes about abuse in a rest home. Since no actual damage was done, nothing seemed to be missing at Pine Hollow, she was released with a warning to let the police do police work.

Back at the house, Marion opened her cell phone to call the police. She knew it was too early for a missing person report, but perhaps they could keep an eye out. She dialed 9-1-1.

"911. What's your emergency?"

Marion glanced out the window and saw Amanda emerge from a police cruiser, wave goodbye to the driver, and limp up the path toward the house.

"Well, that was quick. Thank you," she said and snapped her cell closed.

"Don't even ask," Amanda said as she dragged herself into the living room. "I need a shower."

Marion stood, lips pressed tightly together. She knew the story would unfold in its own time. She walked into the kitchen and cast a glance at the face in the middle of the painting that still lay askew on the kitchen table. *Something familiar about it*, she thought and walked into her room.

"Might as well drop me off at Pine Hollow so I can pick up my car before our local boys in blue impound it," Amanda said after her shower.

"Is that what this was about? They found your car?"

"No, it's just how they found me. They wanted to charge me with breaking and entering until I explained about the alcohol inks, the faces, and the missing woman. Now they think I'm a crackpot, too."

"Too?" Marion said, casting a quick glance at Amanda.

"Apparently, they remember you," Amanda said with a shrug. "I guess we have a reputation to maintain." Amanda turned her head to toward the window. "Could work to our advantage," she murmured.

"Thanks. See you later," Amanda called after Marion dropped her off at her car. She flexed her ankle a couple of times before she started the engine. Painful, but doable.

She pulled into the parking lot at Starbucks. Her heart raced as she scanned the customers on the other side of the plate glass. Jeri sat at a table for two, back from the window. She watched as Jeri lifted an oversized cup to her lips. *I want you*, Amanda thought.

She hobbled up to the counter, ordered a cappuccino, then slowly tried to look cool as she sauntered to Jeri's table—no easy trick with a bum ankle.

"Hey," she said. She pulled a chair out and sat down. "I'm Amanda from your alcohol inks class—

"Amanda, of course, I remember *exactly* who you are." Jeri smiled her greeting. "Good to see you." She extended her hand, and Amanda took it. Jeri covered Amanda's hand with her own and gave a squeeze.

Blood rushed from Amanda's heart up to her neck and flooded her face.

"Amanda. Cappuccino," the woman at the register bellowed.

Amanda slowly withdrew her hand and stood.

"Let me get that for you," Jeri smiled.

When she'd settled back in, Jeri said, "So, what happened to your leg?" She leaned forward, her breasts resting on the table. Her eyes invited Amanda in.

"Late night accident," Amanda muttered.

"Yet willing to come out to chat with me," Jeri replied. "I'm flattered." Her voice was smooth as honey. So how can I be of service?" Jeri's eyes hinted at much more than an answer to any alcohol ink question Amanda might have.

For a moment, Amanda had no idea what her question was. She shook herself back into some semblance of conscientiousness and said, "You remember how you said pictures might emerge from our paintings, things that we didn't intentionally put there?"

Jeri nodded.

"My roommate—we're just friends, we're not involved or anything . . ." *God, why did I say that? I look like an idiot.* "Marion . . . from class. She had a face emerge in her painting."

"Ah, yes, that happens."

"This face belonged to an elderly woman who has gone missing from a care facility, just this week. We compared it to the picture in the paper," Amanda said. "Don't you think that's odd?"

Jeri sat back slowly. Her eyes narrowed, her face blanched, and her mouth was a rigid line.

Curious, Amanda watched this transformation but said nothing.

After a somewhat uncomfortable silence, Jeri answered. "We humans like to ascribe meaning to things." Her voice seemed strained. She looked at the table, not at Amanda. "We like to make sense of the mysteries of life. Sometimes our eyes tell us what our brain wants to hear."

Jeri took a deep breath, leaned forward, and took both of Amanda's hands in her own. "When I saw you in class, I just knew you were someone with a fabulous, creative imagination." She smiled; her perfect white teeth sparkled. "You can't imagine how exciting that is."

Again, Amanda felt a blush creep up to her spine.

"It's like finding a kindred spirit," Jeri said. She blinked her long lashes. "And," she lowered her voice, "I'm glad to hear your roommate is just a roommate."

Amanda's jaw went slack. *Jeri was interested? Available?*

Jeri sat back in her chair, glanced at her watch, and said, "Oh, I didn't realize it was so late. I have another appointment. Will you excuse me?" She beamed her smile at Amanda. "I'll see you in class next week."

Jeri scooted her chair back and left. Amanda sat, flummoxed, and stared at her cold cappuccino. *What just happened?*

Chapter Five

"After last week, it will be good to get back to some semblance of normal," Marion said as they entered the classroom.

Amanda set her bag of art supplies on the table, scanned the room for an early sighting of Jeri, and then checked her watch.

The din of socializing dropped to a whisper as the women settled in. A jolly-looking woman, much like Mrs. Butterworth on the syrup bottle, stood at the head of the room. She clapped her hands, and the room fell silent.

"Good morning, ladies," she beamed. "I'm Sylvia Rogers, and I'll be your instructor this morning. Jeri Kay has been called away." She brought her hands together in a loud clap.

"Wait. . . What?" Amanda groaned. Her perky, saved-for-Jeri smile vanished. Her adorable outfit worn for naught. "But she said . . ." Amanda was acutely aware she hadn't shared with Marion her meeting with Jeri. She could imagine Marion's judgment about crossing boundaries between students and teachers, about Amanda being so much older, and perhaps, not in Jeri's league.

Marion reached over and patted her arm. "It will be okay," she mouthed.

"We're beginning with a YouTube video on how to use our brushes. Then, we'll give it a try," she said, once again clapping her hands in enthusiasm.

"What's with this clapping thing?" Amanda mumbled. "If she does that one more time, I'm going to throw paint on her."

"Now, now," Marion soothed. "We can't all be Jeri Kay."

After the video, they dropped little puddles of ink on their papers and dabbed at them with various brushes. The class created things vaguely resembling trees, leaves, and flowers. Manipulating the ink was a bit like herding cats, but after half an hour, Marion produced a rather lovely likeness to a field of flowers.

Amanda's efforts resembled blobs of ink into which brushes had been smooshed. She sighed heavily, crumpled her paper, and pushed her chair back from the table.

At the break, she sought out Sylvia.

"So, did Jeri say how long she'd be away?" Amanda asked.

"No." Another clap. "It was very last-minute and no real information other than she wouldn't be in," Sylvia said. She had a worried look on her Mrs. Butterworth's face. "These adjunct teachers . . ." she said with a *tsk*, letting her opinion hang unspoken in the air.

"Are you doing research on the Pine Hollow Retirement Home?" Marion asked. "It's curious the way it shut down after only two years in operation."

"Actually, I'm doing a search on Jeri Kay." Amanda tapped several keys on her keyboard. "I don't have a good feeling about her absence today." *See you in class*, Jeri had said.

Amanda gently lifted the calico cat who had just decided to take a nap on the keys. She sat him on the floor and blew on the keys. Cat hair scattered like thin feathers.

Marion shook her head.

"I wonder if the two are connected," Amanda said.

"Jeri Kay and the retirement home? Why would they have any connection?"

Because she had a strange reaction when I told her about the face in the painting and the missing woman, Amanda thought. "Call it a hunch," she said, distracted.

Marion took their lunch dishes into the kitchen.

"Huh," Amanda said. "This is interesting. Jeri Kay, AKA Marilyn Doud, has a string of addresses from Maine, to Florida, Utah, Nevada, and now, in California."

"I've heard those artistic types can be a little unstable," Marion called from the kitchen. "Doud. Why does that name sound familiar?"

"Let's see what I can bring up from her personal background," Amanda mumbled. She tapped her way through several URLs.

Marion sat down in an overstuffed chair by the window, book in hand.

"Seems she's worked as a weight trainer and a personal coach. No wonder she looked so fit." Amanda felt a rush of warmth as she recalled Jeri standing in front of the class that first day. She fanned herself with a magazine from the side table next to her computer. "Thought I was done with these hot flashes," she muttered.

"Can you find out anything about her family with your magic internet search powers?"

"Not much available," Amanda replied. "Looks like she has a sister. There's a post by a Marlene Dowdy of the two of them from a few years back. Must be a vacation snapshot—Bay Harbor. No date. Jeri Kay's hair was black then."

"Marlene?" Marion said.

"Yes. Why?"

Marion set her book aside and stood behind Amanda. "Can you do a search on Pine Hollow—any follow-up articles on the closing? The name Marlene is sticking in my mind."

"Looks like they haven't taken their website down yet," Amanda said clicking the keys. "Owner's name. Marlene Dowdy." She scrolled down the page to a picture of Pine Hollow's director.

Marion gasped. Her hand flew to her chest as she leaned in for a closer look. "Could that be?"

"The second face in your painting?" Amanda said.

"I'm not sure," Marion said. "The snapshot was from years ago, but don't you think there's a similarity?"

The women exchanged an *ah-ha* look.

"Seems a little close for comfort, wouldn't you say?" Marion ran her hand through her hair. "Marilyn Doud and Marlene Dowdy, sisters? Maybe Marilyn changed her name from Dowdy to Doud to get a little distance from her sis. And then changed her name again to Jeri Kay, for a lot more distance."

"Interesting theory," Amanda said. "But why would she want to disassociate herself from her sister—if, indeed, that's what she was doing by changing her name?" She crooked her head at Marion.

"I don't know. It might have something to do with the care facility." Marion threw her hands up in surrender. "This is giving me a headache. Let's go out for a hot-fudge sundae."

"I hate traffic," Amanda complained as she inched her way through town toward Mad Dog Ice Cream Parlour.

"You could call on your guides for a parking space," Marion reminded her.

"My guides don't do parking spaces—they're more into 'warnings.' Parking seems to be your guide's specialty."

"Okay." Marion sighed.

They circled the lot once again.

"Bingo!" Amanda said with a cheer. She pulled into a space that had opened right in front of the ice cream parlor. "How do they do that?"

"Don't know. It seems limited to parking spaces though. Doesn't do a thing for traffic."

The afternoon sweltered, and the air conditioning was a balm as they joined the line at Mad Dog.

Amanda reached the order desk. "Two hot-fudge sundaes," she said to the clerk. Then turned to Marion, "Right?"

Marion stood statue-still before a tub of black licorice ice cream.

"Marion?" Amanda touched Marion's shoulder. "Uh oh," she mumbled. "She's having 'a moment.' Can't take her anywhere," she said to no one in particular. Amanda turned to the clerk, confirmed their order, then turned back to Marion. She clapped her hands like the crack of a whip alongside Marion's ear.

Marion jolted back, blinked several times, placed her hand over her heart, and took a deep breath.

"Go sit down," Amanda said. "I'll bring these over." She pointed to a vacant table near the window.

Amanda brought the sundaes and glasses of water and pushed one of the glasses toward Marion. "Drink," she said. "You're probably dehydrated. So, what did you see?"

"Death," said Marion. She placed the cool glass on her forehead and rolled it back and forth. "The dark licorice snapped me into a vision of a hole in the ground somewhere in the woods."

"Do you think it's connected to the case?" They'd been using the euphemism, 'the case' since all the odd bits and pieces lately seemed linked together.

Marion gave her a 'you're-trying-my-patience' stare. "Why else would I see death images as I stare at ice cream?"

"Don't have to get testy," Amanda shot back. She took a big, gooey bite of her hot fudge sundae. Chocolate drizzled down her chin.

Marion dipped the tip of her napkin in her water glass and swiped at the chocolate.

Anyone watching would have thought they were a quirky pair who had been together forever.

"You haven't touched your ice cream," Amanda said, gesturing with her spoon.

"I'm afraid I've lost my appetite." Marion slid her sundae across the table where it was welcomed by an appetite that knew no limit. She gazed out the window where passers by intermingled unknowingly with earthbound souls who turned their beseeching stares her way. They always found her.

Chapter Six

"So, what do we know?" Marion asked as they sat in front of Amanda's computer.

"You mean as opposed to what do we think?"

"Yes. We know Pine Hollow has been vacated."

"We think," added Amanda, "there was abuse. At least, one of the residents tried to notify someone."

"We know Esther Hart 'went missing' before the facility closed," Marion said.

"We think Esther was the writer of the note and the first face that called out for your help from your painting," Amanda said.

"We know Marlene Dowdy was the owner of Pine Hollow; she has also 'gone missing.' Her face was the second image to emerge in your painting. Your serve," she said as if volleying over to Amanda.

"I want to be the 'we-know person.' I'm tired of 'we think,'" Amanda groused.

"Fine."

"We know Jeri is related to Marlene Dowdy, right?" Amanda offered.

"That's still a 'we think,'" Marion said.

"Rats."

"Jeri may have changed her name to distance herself from her sister," Marion said. "But we're not sure why we think that."

"Do we also think Jeri's sudden absence from class has something to do with the missing Marlene?"

"I thought you were tired of being the 'we think,'" Marion said. She did a slow owl-blink at Amanda. "But yes, I guess we should search there next. What can we find out about Marlene Dowdy's background?"

"Other than Pine Hollow, not much comes up," Amanda said. "Let me make a few calls to my sources. No reason to think the sisters moved together, but no reason not to, either."

Amanda spent the next several hours on the telephone with her aforementioned "sources," a collection of ex-cops, undercover detectives, newspaper reporters, secretaries, a handful of dispatchers, and a sprinkling of derelicts.

"Well, color me embarrassed," Amanda said as Marion cleared clutter from the table for dinner. "The lesbians will take away my pink triangle if this gets out."

Marion stopped with a dinner plate in each hand and looked at Amanda. "Whatever are you talking about?"

"Internalized homophobia. We assumed because Marlene and Marilyn shared a last name, they were sisters."

"Uh-huh," Marion said with a shrug.

"Wrong. They're married." She looked up at Marion whose mouth had puckered in confusion and eyebrows had inched up on her forehead.

"Jeri and the owner of Pine Hollow are married?" Marion spoke each word as if she tasted it, trying to identify its flavor.

Amanda nodded. "Or, at least they were. One source said Marlene worked as a private caregiver several years ago and was held on suspicion of murdering one of her elderly clients. They couldn't prove anything, and the woman was never found, so they had to release her."

"Oh, dear God! Jeri is married to a murderer?" Marion sat the plates down with a *clank*. "Maybe we shouldn't get involved in this, after all."

Just then, Amanda's cell rang with the first few notes of Beethoven's "Fifth Symphony."

"Amanda here," she answered. Her eyes widened. She looked at Marion then quickly looked away, covered the mouthpiece and said, "I'll take this outside." In response to the words, "Amanda, it's Jeri. Don't say anything." Amanda rushed out the door to the far end of the backyard.

Amanda hunkered down over her phone and whispered, "Jeri, are you all right? Are you safe?" She cast a glance back at the house. Marion was nowhere in sight. Beyond her worries about Jeri, Amanda noticed a little tingle in her pelvis at the sound of Jeri's voice.

"I don't know people around here, and I didn't know who else to call," Jeri said. Her voice was tight, hesitant. "I probably shouldn't involve you, but I felt we had, or could have, a connection . . . at coffee . . . Do you know what I mean?" The tightness broke into sobs.

"Yes. You're right," Amanda said. Pleasure washed over her for a moment. *I knew there was something there.* "I've been so worried about you." She thought back to Jeri's look of discomfort around the painting, the face, and the care home, followed by her absence at the next class with no explanation.

"I'm in trouble, Amanda, and I can't go to the police. I don't know what to do."

"Can you meet me at the lake? There's a bench at the entrance—"

"I don't want my car to be seen around here," Jeri said. "I've sort of gone into hiding. Oh, this is such a mess."

"I know, I know," Amanda said sympathetically.

"What?" Jeri's voice went from frightened to suspicious. "What do you mean you know?"

"I've done some research. When you disappeared, I got scared. I started digging around—"

She heard Jeri gasp.

"No, no, it's okay," Amanda said. "You're safe with me."

"What do you mean, 'digging around?'"

"I do some sleuthing, unofficially. This is about Marlene and the Pine Hollow Care Center, isn't it?"

Silence followed.

"Jeri, are you still there?" Amanda peered into her phone as if she could see through the wireless connection.

"Yes." Jeri paused. "Can you meet me outside of town in half an hour?"

They agreed to meet at the little-used rear entrance of a towering redwood grove.

"Gotta go out for a little while," Amanda called over her shoulder to Marion as she rushed through the house, grabbed her keys, and left with a bang of the front door.

"What about dinner?" Marion asked the empty space.

The sun set as Amanda pulled next to the only other car in the small parking lot. Jeri Kay sat scrunched down in the driver seat of her SUV. The bill of her baseball cap shaded her face. Each woman opened their car door slowly, cautiously—Jeri surveilling the surroundings for safety, Amanda not wanting to startle her.

"There's a bench just a little way up the path. We can talk there," Amanda said.

Jeri followed her up the path. "You're still limping," she noted. "What happened?"

"Sleuthing injury. Long story," Amanda said.

"So?" Jeri asked when they'd situated themselves on the bench.

A smile quirked the corner of Amanda's lips. "What I *think* I know is Marlene is your partner. She was in some deep legal trouble on the east coast but got out of it for lack of evidence."

Jeri inhaled quickly. Her eyebrows raised in alarm.

"*Was* my partner," Jeri clarified. "The woman is crazy, a homicidal maniac. I left her in Nevada, but she found me here earlier this year and moved in."

"She had something to do with the disappearance of Esther Hart, didn't she?"

Jeri paled and seemed to cave in on herself. She stared at the ground, mute.

Amanda reached out and took Jeri's heavy, lifeless hand. "Can you tell me if Esther is still alive?" She felt a shudder pass through Jeri. "Listen, if Marlene did something, you're not to blame. Do you understand? It's not your fault."

Jeri took a deep breath but said nothing.

"Come on, Jeri, talk to me."

"I buried her," Jeri said in a small voice.

For a moment, Amanda had an up-close-and-personal experience of the phrase, "chilled to the bone." She swallowed hard, forced air into her lungs. "*You* buried Esther?"

"And others," Jeri said. "I mean, you can't just leave them lying around, you know. Someone had to clean up her messes. If I didn't help, she would have killed me as well."

Oh my God, oh my God, oh my God, Amanda chanted inside her head. *Marlene is a serial killer. And Jeri buried them*! She looked at Jeri who had large tears slowly rolling down her cheeks. Her lips pressed tightly together.

Even aware of Jeri's darkness, Amanda's heartstrings tangled around the intensely attractive woman who sat before her.

"Will you help me?" Jeri asked after a moment.

"Do you know where Marlene is now?"

Jeri shook her head slowly. "She goes away after she makes the kill—after she knows I've gotten rid of the body. But she always comes back, always finds me." She turned a beseeching look on Amanda. "You see why I can't involve the police, right? I'd be thrown in prison as an accessory to murder."

"We need help," Amanda said. She saw Jeri bristle. She knew this might be a bad idea but was willing to take the risk. "We need my roommate, Marion. She helps me solve crimes without involving the police. You can trust her, I swear."

"No! Absolutely not. You can't tell anyone. If you do, I'll disappear." Jeri yanked her hand from Amanda's and jumped to her feet.

"Okay. All right. Don't panic," Amanda said as she grabbed Jeri's wrist anchoring her for the moment. "You'll get through this."

How she would get through it? Amanda didn't know. She sat quietly for a moment and considered her options.

"To keep you safe, we need to know where Marlene is," Amanda said. She looked at Jeri who stared at the ground. "Turning this over to the police is not a good idea, I agree—at least, not yet. But you and I can't do this on our own."

Amanda made a quick mental pro and con list for what she was about to suggest. She could predict Marion's reaction to this, which she weighed against the possibility of her help in finding Marlene.

"My roommate has special psychic skills and might be able to help locate her."

Again, she glanced at Jeri whose hands were gripped so tightly her knuckles were white.

"Once we've found her, then we can decide what to do. Okay?"

Jeri nodded, her reluctance obvious.

Chapter Seven

After dinner, they huddled in Amanda's cozy living room. The teapot whistled on the stove in the kitchen. "Start from the beginning, and tell me everything," Marion said.

"Wait, wait," Amanda replied. She bustled into the kitchen and returned with three steaming cups of herbal tea. "Okay, go."

Jeri drew a hesitant breath, let it out in a long sigh, looked at each woman, and then said, "You have to promise me you won't go to the police with any of this. My life is on the line."

Marion set her teacup back down on the steamer trunk that served as a coffee table. "Jeri Kay, you do understand keeping this secret would potentially make us accessories to murder. In fact, we may need their help in finding Marlene. I don't want to wind up in prison beside her."

"I thought you had special psychic skills to find people," Jeri said with a trickle of tears running down her cheeks. She blinked her glistening eyes at Marion.

"Well, sometimes that's true. But what if we found her? Then what? What would we do with her? She's a serial killer, for God sake. I mean, no offense," Marion said.

Jeri's eyes were downcast, sullen. She seemed to warm her hands with her teacup. "I know. I know. If the police find her, she'll wind up in prison for sure—

which, of course, is where she should be. But, what about me? I aided her. What does that make me?"

"Guilty as sin," Amanda said and then slapped her hand over her mouth. "Sorry . . . just sort of slipped out."

"But it's true," Jeri said miserably. "I'll be in prison right alongside her."

"No, not necessarily. There are extenuating circumstances," Marion said. "Like you thought she'd kill you if you didn't help her. And you didn't actually do the killing, right?"

"Maybe you could plead Stockholm Syndrome or something," Amanda offered.

Marion reached over and took Jeri's hand. "Listen, dear, let us help you find her . . . without involving the police. Then we'll decide what to do once we've located her."

"Once we've found her, maybe you can split—go into hiding or something," Amanda said.

Marion shot her a look

"No, really," Amanda said. "The police think we're just crazy old women anyway. We could tell them where she is, what's she's done, but stay quiet about how we know. Let them follow up from there. No need to even involve Jeri."

"But she *is* involved," Marion argued. She squeezed the woman's hand and looked into her eyes. "You're going to carry this around with you for a lifetime unless you choose this moment to take responsibility for your part. We'll do everything we can to help."

Jeri sank back against the futon. "I'm so tired of running. Tired of living in fear," she said. "Thank you." She looked at Marion, then at Amanda. "Thank you for being willing to help, for being my friends. I've been alone with this for so many years."

"Why don't you get some sleep, and we'll start fresh in the morning," Marion suggested.

"Yes," Amanda agreed. "The futon folds out into a bed. I'll get a pillow and some quilts."

After tucking Jeri in, Amanda and Marion retired to their own rooms. Thoroughly exhausted, they slept soundly through the night.

Marion awoke just after 7:00 a.m. She stretched, glanced out the window at the sunny day, and listened to a mockingbird for a few moments. *Ah, the simplicity of life after a good night's sleep.* There was no noise from the kitchen—*Amanda must have slept in as well.*

Marion padded down the hall, used the bathroom, and wandered quietly into the living room to check on Jeri. Marion blinked in surprise. She scanned the room then cocked her head for any sounds of movement. Nothing. No Jeri Kay. Her backpack was gone. The quilts neatly folded on the end of the futon, and the pillows rested next to them.

"Jeri?" Marion called.

Nothing.

Marion went into the kitchen. "Jeri?"

No sign of Jeri, not even an empty teacup. She scanned the backyard. Nothing still.

"*She's in bed with Amanda!*" Marion thought exasperated. *Didn't Amanda have any sense?* She headed straight for Amanda's room and knocked lightly.

Within a minute, a groggy Amanda opened the bedroom door.

"You slept with her?" Marion whispered. "What were you thinking?"

Amanda yawned and rubbed the sleep from her eyes with her fists. "What in the name of the Goddess are you talking about?" she said.

"Oh dear," Marion muttered. She glanced into Amanda's room and felt a sense of dread coil in her chest.

"Jeri Kay. She's gone!"

"Oh, she probably just went out for coffee or something. A good night's sleep didn't seem to do much for your nerves," Amanda replied.

Marion went straight for the living room and glanced at the driveway. "Your car's gone too!"

"Well, you didn't expect her to walk into town, did you? Amanda said as she entered the room.

"I swear! You are blinded by that woman." Marion shook her head in frustration. Her voice raised in pitch and volume. "Don't you see what's happened? She dumped this big mess in our lives and then ran out so she wouldn't have to take any responsibility."

"See? *This* is why I was hesitant to involve you. You overreact," Amanda said. She flung her arms in the air.

"For God sake, the woman stole your car!" Marion yelled. "I'm sorry if I'm not reasonable about this." She stormed out of the kitchen, into her room, and slammed the door behind her.

Amanda walked into the living room. No, she would not look around. No, she didn't believe the heirloom crystal vase on the shelf was be gone, nor her wallet that she'd left atop the television. She sat heavily on the futon, stared at the floor, and wondered what to do next.

Chapter Eight

"Well, I can't just hide out in my room forever." Marion sighed. "Besides, it's lunchtime." She took a deep breath, squared her shoulders, and marched through the living room to the kitchen. What she didn't expect—what she really didn't know how to handle—was Amanda, curled up in a fetal position on the futon, sobbing as though her world had come to an end.

A tsunami of guilt hit Marion. She rushed over to the futon, sank to her knees beside Amanda, took her Kleenex-drenched hand, and said, "Oh, Amanda, I'm so very sorry. I should have never spoken to you like that. I was just upset. Can you ever forgive me?"

Amanda looked up through red, weepy eyes and sobbed, "You were right. I'm such an old fool." She choked on her tears and spent a grueling moment coughing and trying to catch her breath. "I'm never going to love again," she wailed.

Marion helped her to a sitting position, patted her back, and handed her the box of tissues.

"I'm a lousy judge of character. No wonder women use me then leave. I'm such a patsy," she said through a fresh gale of tears.

"There, there," Marion said, trying to soothe Amanda's obviously broken heart. "That's not true. You just love passionately. Sometimes it clouds your judgment." What she didn't say was how she envied someone who could love so easily, trust so freely. She could barely admit that to herself.

She rubbed slow circles on Amanda's back. "Maybe you're right," she said. "Maybe she'll come home this evening."

"*Nooo*," Amanda wailed. "My wallet is gone. My great-aunt's crystal vase is gone. How could I be so stupid to trust her? You *knew*. You knew all along."

"Oh, honey, I'm just a natural skeptic. She was pretty convincing, though. How could someone like her—a gorgeous art teacher at the JC—be on the wrong side of the law?"

Amanda shot her a sardonic look. "What are we going to do?" Amanda's face looked pasty, bloated, drained of color.

"First thing we're going to do is call the bank and close your account. Then we'll cancel all your credit cards and file a police report. At least, it will slow Jeri down," Marion said.

"We can't report Jeri. What will we tell the police? We were harboring a fugitive from justice, and she ripped us off? Big surprise." Amanda wrung her hands.

"Listen, they think we both have a few screws loose anyway. Let's say you fell asleep on the futon, and someone came in and stole your wallet, car keys, and the vase. You never lock the door, so it's at least feasible," Marion said. "Then there will be a report on file if any fraudulent charges are made, or the car is spotted."

Marion rubbed her temples in little circles. "Oh, no. Look at the time. We have ten minutes before we have to leave for class."

"I'm not going back to class. I'm done with art. Forever." Amanda's bottom lip quivered. "I'll stay here and make those calls. You go on to class. Really, I'll be okay. It's good to have something to do."

"Wait a minute," Marion's voice bristled. "You can't just bail out on me. The only reason I took this class is because of you."

"And thank goodness for that, right? Your art has produced clues to a murder. My art looks like a pig sty."

Marion opened her mouth to protest, closed it, and headed out the door.

Later that morning, Amanda heard a loud knock at the front door. "Come in," Amanda yelled from the kitchen. She met Officer Maxwell in the living room.

"Your door was unlocked," Officer Maxwell, face grim and no trace of smile-wrinkles, pointed a finger at Amanda.

Amanda studied the officer's stern face. *Occupational hazard*, she thought.

"Um . . . I was expecting you," Amanda said. "I promise I'll lock it from here on. Have a seat." She motioned Officer Maxwell to a side chair.

At the end of the interview, Officer Maxwell summarized, "You woke this morning to find your keys and car were gone. Your wallet and an heirloom vase missing from the living room. You have no idea who may have taken these items. Nothing else was missing. Your door was unlocked overnight, and there was no forced entry. Is that correct?"

"Yes ma'am," Amanda said. "Are you going to dust for prints?"

"We don't do that for burglaries anymore," Officer Maxwell said. "I'll put out a report on the missing items, but I have to tell you, aside from the car, it doesn't look good for recovery. You'll need to call your bank and—"

"Yes, yes. I've already done all that," Amanda said.

"And lock your door," the officer said with a raised eyebrow as she let herself out.

"What's this world coming to," Amanda mumbled, "when you have to lock your door against people you thought you knew?"

What if Jeri came back? She blocked that thought and rechecked the front lock.

An hour and a half later, Marion sat at the kitchen table studying the Yupo paper spread in front of her. Her painting was a vague impression of a winter forest done in brown, mushroom, and gray.

"You missed an excellent class," she said. "We're learning how to paint trees by manipulating the ink and blending in other colors. It's very challenging." She made a frame of her thumbs and hands and glided it over the surface of the painting, highlighting various segments, as she cocked her head to the left and the right.

Marion looked up and saw Amanda across from her devouring a triple-decker peanut butter, banana, and marshmallow sandwich. As if Amanda hadn't heard a word Marion had said, her eyes look glazed, and she seemed galaxies away.

"Oh, for God sake, Amanda. You're not turning to food to fill the emotional void Jeri Kay left, are you?"

"You've been watching too much *Dr. Phil*," Amanda said around her mouthful of sandwich. She wiped her mouth with the back of her hand and turned her attention to a stack of chocolate chip cookies.

Marion shook her head. Feeling abandoned in their once-shared interest in the arts, she sighed as Amanda took her stack of cookies and walked into the living room.

I will not let her drag me down. Marion uncapped a vial of isopropyl alcohol and grabbed a cotton ball to tidy up a smear toward the base of a tree in the center of the painting.

"Dammit," she swore in frustration, as much at the enlarging smear where the alcohol rearranged the ink molecules, as at Amanda. She studied the mess she'd just made.

"Oh, no . . ." She jammed her chair back so quickly that she had to grab the table to keep from toppling over. "Amanda, come look!" she called to the living room. There was no response.

With a groan, Marion noted the unmistakable outline of a grave cluttered with detritus in the middle of the stand of trees. "Amanda!"

Marion stalked into the living room. No Amanda. The front door stood ajar. "Oh, great. This is just great," Marion said.

Marion made herself soup and a sandwich for dinner and called it an early night. Somewhere around 10:00, she heard Amanda slip in quietly and go into her room. Marion harrumphed, turned over, and went back to sleep.

In her dreamscape, she saw the woods she had painted earlier and felt a terrible foreboding as the grave came into focus.

The leaves and twigs covering it shifted. Clots of earth and puffs of dust fell to the side. A white, mottled hand pushed up and curled over the edge of the grave. Marion tried to scream, but no sound came. It was as if her throat was paralyzed.

A shoulder rose out of the dirt, followed by the head of the old woman who had gone missing. Wisps of white hair left large exposed patches of the skull. She looked at Marion with hollow eyes. Cracked lips and chipped teeth formed the words, "Help me."

Oh, my God, Marion thought. She needed to run. She needed to get in her car and drive. Keep driving until she felt she was safe. Her heart thumped in her chest, and her entire body tensed. "Oh, dear God, I can't move," Marion muttered.

A hand grabbed Marion and shook her. Marion screamed and struck at the apparition.

"Stop it. Wake up, Marion. It's just me," Amanda said as she blocked a thrashing arm. "You were having a nightmare." She clicked on the bedside lamp.

Panting, heart pounding, Marion managed to sit up. Her nightshirt was soaked with sweat. She clung to Amanda in desperation. "Don't leave me alone with this," she begged.

Amanda held Marion and slowly rocked her until Marion's breathing calmed.

"I'm sorry," Amanda said. "I've been acting like an idiot. I've been so caught up in my own misery; I've lost focus of the bigger picture. I won't leave you alone, I promise. Your nightmare was about the case, wasn't it?"

Marion nodded. "It was awful. Esther's corpse came right up out of the ground—her grave showed up in today's painting. Amanda, I think she's buried in the woods, not far from here."

"Okay. It's after midnight, but first thing after breakfast, let's put on our hiking boots and see if we can locate the area by the picture you painted. There may be other details we didn't notice. Do you think you can get back to sleep?"

Marion shook her head.

"Do you want me to stay with you?"

Marion nodded and scooted to the edge of her double bed. Amanda hefted her bulk beside Marion, who spooned close to her. Before long, both snored gently.

Hours later, the sun splashed through the crack beneath the blind. Amanda tried to stretch but found

Marion's knees plastered tightly behind hers. She tried to loosen herself from Marion's arm now slung over Amanda's middle, waking Marion in the process.

"What?" Marion mumbled.

"I just want you to know I don't make a habit of sleeping with straight women," Amanda said.

Marion swatted her on the hip and turned over on her back. "What time is it?" She rubbed a crick in her neck.

"7:00. Time for breakfast. We've got work to do this morning."

The phone rang, and Marion answered it while Amanda pulled on her robe and headed for the kitchen.

"Yes, this is Marion Knox," she said to the caller. "Oh. Well, yes. That's sooner than I'd expected. Okay. Thank you." She set the phone back on the bedside table and looked around the room. Tears pooled, and her bottom lip quivered. She wiped her eyes, blew her nose, and walked into the kitchen.

"Who calls this early? Anything important?" Amanda asked.

"My apartment is ready. I can move back in this week." She sat on a kitchen chair with elbows on the table and rested her chin on her hands.

"Oh," Amanda said. "Well, good, right?" Her voice was hesitant. "A bug-free apartment."

"I'm sure you're ready to reclaim your peace and quiet," Marion said, looking over at Amanda.

Neither said anything more.

Amanda sat two mugs of coffee, two ceramic bowls, and a box of cereal on the table. Marion retrieved the milk from the fridge and sugar from the cabinet. It was their morning ritual. They looked at one another.

"I don't want to go," Marion said at the same time that Amanda blurted, "I don't want you to go."

Amanda smiled. "I've kinda gotten accustomed to your face," she said with a sheepish grin.

"I didn't know I was lonely until I moved in here," Marion admitted to herself as well as to Amanda. "Do you think we'd drive each other nuts if we made this a permanent arrangement?"

"Probably," Amanda said. "Call your landlord and give your thirty-day notice. We'll start moving your stuff tomorrow."

They raised their coffee mugs in a silent toast to their friendship.

"We probably should have thought this through a little more before calling the movers," Amanda said as a burly man carted her futon out and tossed it in the back of his pickup truck. The signage on the vehicle read, Two Guys With A Truck.

"They were the only ones available in the next three weeks," Marion said.

Amanda heaved a sigh as the second mover, with her old Formica kitchen table balanced on his back, shoved past her on the porch steps.

"I really appreciate you making space for my furniture," Marion said. "I know you were attached to your things."

Amanda looked away as her paisley-paper hanging lantern joined the other Salvation Army donations. "Someone's going to love that," she said under her breath. She swiped at her eye and removed the threat of a tear. "I wouldn't do this for just anyone, you know."

"I know." Marion took Amanda's hand and gave it a squeeze. "I think my furniture will look good in here. It's . . ."

"More tasteful? Grown up? Of this era?" She bit off her words.

"Just newer," Marion said.

"No!" Amanda hollered as the two men carried her steamer trunk out the front door. She stamped her foot. "Turn around and take that right back."

Chapter Nine

Amanda washed the breakfast dishes while Marion tidied up the kitchen. A loud rap on the front door startled them both.

"I'll get it," Marion said. She peered out the front window before going to the door and saw a faded blue VW parked in the driveway.

"Amanda, come quick. It's your car."

"Jeri?"

Both women collided at the front door. Amanda opened it to see Officer Bette Maxwell's cheerless face staring at her.

"Found your car," she said, pointing toward the VW. "Parked at the airport. The thief probably hopped a flight out of here. Best we can do," she said.

"That's wonderful," Marion replied. "Are you going to look for the other stolen items?" she asked.

Officer Bette squinted her eyes and shook her head slowly. "You're lucky you got your car. Best to get yourself another wallet and replace your cards. The vase? Don't hold your breath." She handed Amanda her keys, turned, and departed to the waiting squad car.

"Thank you," Amanda called after her. "Personality of a rock," she muttered to Marion as she closed the door.

"Well, how timely," Marion said. "Now we can take your car to do our 'womanhunt.'"

"My car would be more recognizable since it's the one she took. If we're looking to be invisible, we should take your Honda."

"Okay, let's get dressed and get us some criminals," Marion said. She rubbed her hands together gleefully.

When they reconvened in the living room, Marion was dressed in blue jeans with a gray trench coat over a black sweater. Amanda sported a fuchsia T-shirt and green leggings.

Marion gaped. "I thought we were trying to be invisible."

Amanda went to the hall closet, pulled out a pair of camouflage fatigues and slipped them on over her ensemble. "We are."

Before they left, Marion grabbed the ink painting and scanned it for any details they may have missed.

"It looks like any old generic forest or timber," Amanda said.

"That's it!" Marion said. "It's more timber than a forest. The trees are thinner and closer together."

"That rules out the redwood grove," Amanda said. "But, there's the timberland, about a mile down the road on the other side of town."

"Wait . . . What's that?" Marion pointed to the corner of the painting.

"It looks like some kind of signpost. You didn't paint it there on purpose?"

Marion shook her head. "Well, it's somewhere to start anyway."

The fog was thick and obscured their view. As the car crept by the timber area, the women peered into the trees for any hint of where to begin. Marion made a U-turn, put the car in neutral, and quietly glided into a pull-off area in a patch of dirt. They reviewed their mission.

"Okay, we're looking for a gravesite, a crazy murderer, and her on-the-lam cohort," Amanda said.

"And some sort of signpost," Marion added.

They shrugged and smiled at each other.

"Well, we've had less to work with in the past," Amanda said. "Let's go."

As quiet as possible, they exited the car and stole across the road. Amanda scanned the woods.

"Here," she said in a whisper. "A deer trail— faint, but I say we give it a try."

The fog dampened the sound of their footsteps as they picked their way among the trees in search of anything resembling a hole big enough to contain a body.

"Stop!" Marion said in a loud whisper. She threw out her arm blocking Amanda.

"Geez, scare me half to death, will ya," Amanda said. She looked in the direction Marion pointed.

A dilapidated, hand-painted wooden sign hung at an angle from a short post pounded into the soil. They worked their way closer until they could read the faded-red lettering. *Keep Out*!

"Yeah, like that's going to stop a crazy murderer," Amanda whispered.

"It's the sign in the painting," Marion said. "I think we're in the right place." They stood quietly, gazing through the trees.

"Let's go," Amanda said.

They followed the deer trail deeper into the timber where the ground felt spongy.

Marion put her arm out again, this time even slower. "We're close. I can feel it."

"Just warning you, if I see a hand poking up out of a hole, I'm gonna scream," Amanda said.

They proceeded, carefully scanning the ground as they moved.

Several yards off the trail a patch of earth appeared to have been dug up and then covered over with leaves, twigs, and branches.

"That's it, isn't it?" Amanda said in a hushed voice.

"I think so," Marion said.

Both women stood their ground.

"I don't think I can do this." Amanda stepped back. "Maybe we should just go home and call the police. Let them handle it."

"And tell them what? We found a hole in the woods?" Marion crossed her arms. "I don't think so. We've come this far, we might as well check it out."

"Maybe we're wrong. Maybe a hunter killed a deer off-season or something and buried it out here," Amanda said.

Marion shot her a skeptical look.

Amanda shrugged.

"We owe it to Esther Hart to at least check to see if this is where she wound up," Marion said with more conviction than she felt.

They eased their way through the trees until they were at the edge of the uneven mound of dirt. A twig snapped behind them. Marion gasped and grabbed her heart. Amanda froze.

Another sound, like footsteps, followed. "I'm going to faint," Amanda whispered.

Marion slowly pivoted her body. "Oh, my God," she said and heaved a sigh of relief. "It's a deer."

Amanda exhaled loudly. "Must be the one that got away," she said, glancing back at the disrupted patch of earth.

When they'd recovered, they edged closer to the mound.

"Um, I hate to state the obvious," Amanda said, "but we're not exactly prepared to dig up a grave. We didn't bring a shovel."

Marion looked crestfallen. "That hadn't occurred to me," she said.

"Perhaps we should go back—"

"No," Marion interrupted. "This is a timber. There are tree branches all over the ground. We'll just use what we have." She looked around, took a few steps, and retrieved a sturdy branch.

"Please tell me you're not going to poke it into the hole," Amanda said, grimacing. "What if you hit something?"

"Come on, find a branch, and help me," Marion said. "We'll scrape away the top layer." She shivered as an eerie feeling of ghostliness passed through her and glanced around to see if anyone was watching.

"I must be nuts letting you talk me into this," Amanda muttered. She picked up a long branch, which would allow her some distance from the mound.

As quietly as possible, they began brushing away the detritus until they reached a crumbled layer of dirt. Amanda's branch suddenly seemed immobile, unable to scrape even another inch deeper.

Marion sighed and poked gently around the edges of the hole then worked her way toward the middle. She stopped short, dropped to her knees, and with a shaky hand, brushed at the dirt.

No, no, no. I really don't want to see this, Marion chanted in her mind. Her stomach roiled. She gasped as she uncovered a dirt-encrusted lock of gray hair and jerked her hand back.

Amanda dropped her branch, back-stepped away from the grave, and stared in disbelief. A look of horror paled her face. "That's enough," she said in a strained voice. "Don't go any farther. The police can take it from here."

"You're right. I agree with you," Marion agreed.

"Maybe we should cover her back up," Amanda said. "I mean, so the animals don't . . ." She shuddered.

"Wait." Marion looked up, turned her head from side to side.

"Oh, no. Not something else," Amanda said. "I just can't do something else."

"I smell smoke," Marion said, sniffing the air.

"Campers? Oh, great. We're going to be discovered. They'll think *we* buried the body here. Run!" Amanda spun around.

"Stop," Marion said in a harsh whisper as she grabbed Amanda's arm. "We have to check it out. Maybe they have a cell phone with them, and we can call the police from here. Then we won't have to abandon the grave."

"And maybe it's the people who put her here— did you think about that?"

The fog had begun to lift, giving them a clearer view through the trees. They walked toward a thin plume of black smoke. Ahead, nestled among some fallen trees, was a tent encampment. Blankets were strewn over branches giving a colorful, festive feel to the four tents. An unattended campfire burned low. The smell of coffee wafted toward Marion and Amanda, unleashing a chorus of stomach gurgles.

"Shhh," they said to one another and stepped back behind a tree to watch.

Scratching his crotch then stretching, a man with an untamed beard stepped out of a tent. He shuffled past the fire and into another tent. A small, ragged dog of indeterminate breed bounded through the camp, chasing whatever it is that dogs chase.

Amanda grabbed Marion's arm. "What if the dog smells us and alerts the others?" They took a few steps farther back into the timber and continued to observe.

Moments later, a woman with a hoodie approached the fire. She stirred the embers, added another log, and placed a package wrapped in aluminum foil among the coals. She sat back on a stump near the fire, pulled her hoodie off, and ran her fingers through her short-cropped hair.

Amanda inhaled sharply.

Marion slapped a hand over Amanda's mouth and shook her head in warning. *Don't speak*, she mouthed as Amanda stood wide-eyed, looking at Jeri Kay.

Chapter Ten

Standing as still as the trees that hid them, Amanda and Marion waited for what they suspected would come next.

Moments later, Marlene, former owner of the now-defunct Pine Hollow Care Center, appeared with paper plates and two mugs. She wore dirty overalls, a sweatshirt, and an oversized, ratty coat. She lifted a metal coffee pot from the far side of the campfire, filled their cups, and handed one to Jeri. Jeri unwrapped and dumped the contents of the foil package onto their plates.

Remembering breakfast had been hours ago, Amanda swallowed hard. *What do you suppose they'd do if we just walked up and invited ourselves to breakfast?*

Marion strained forward as if trying to catch their conversation. She nodded a retreat to Amanda, and ever so slowly, they worked their way backward. Making as little noise as possible, they continued until were out of sight of the encampment.

Amanda collapsed against a tree, hand over her heart, and tried to slow her breathing. Marion leaned her shoulder against the same tree and took long, deep breaths.

"I say we get the hell out of here," Amanda said.

Back in town, they parked in front of the local police station.

"Okay," Amanda said. "We could just go in, lay out our story, give them directions, and leave it at that."

"Our story being?" Marion arched her eyebrows.

"We have reason to believe—"

"Based on what?" Marion interrupted. "An ink painting? Intuition? Psychic, ghostly apparitions?"

Amanda sighed and looked out the window.

Just then, a patrol car sped out of the driveway, siren blaring, and shot down the street. Both women scrunched down in their seats.

"Wait a minute," Amanda said. "We're not guilty of anything." She squirmed her way back up.

"Except maybe obstruction of justice, withholding evidence. Aiding and abetting. Must I go on?" Marion pulled herself up behind the wheel. "What if we just stick to what we know?"

"Which is?"

"There's a body buried in the woods. We believe it to be the missing Esther Hart, a resident of the Pine Hollow Care Center. We think two women are responsible for her death. They had a tent encampment yards from the gravesite. One of them is Marlene Dowdy, the former owner of the Pine Hollow Care Center. Here's a map. We suggest you hurry."

"And they'll believe us because, why?" Amanda frowned.

"Because we're going to hand them a map," Marion said as she fished around in her purse for a paper and pen.

Working together, the women constructed a visual map with written instructions, mentioning the deer trail entrance and the wooden signpost.

"They're going to have a million questions for us that we're not going to be able to answer in a way that won't sound like we're crazy," Amanda said, shaking her head.

"The important thing is they send someone out to investigate." Marion folded the map. "If they don't, we take this map to the newspaper."

Chapter Eleven

"Wait over there," the woman behind the thick glass window said through a small speaker hole. "A detective will be with you."

Amanda busied herself looking through a tattered motorcycle magazine while Marion fidgeted next to her.

"You noticed she didn't say a detective would be with us *soon*." Marion unfolded and refolded the map, stood, paced around the waiting area, and returned to her seat. "Surely, we have more than one police detective in this fair city of ours." She glared impatiently at the receptionist who seemed oblivious to non-verbal communication.

About thirty minutes later, they sat across from Detective Madison Bright. The interrogation room was tiny with what Amanda assumed was a one-way mirror. She kept peeking at it, resisting the urge to wave.

"And how is it you two ladies happened upon this grave? Just strolling through the woods, were you? Looking for dead bodies?" There was no hint of a smile on his face.

"At this moment, the details of why we were there are less important than sending someone out to unearth the poor woman," Marion said. "Her daughter would be very distraught to think you ignored our report."

"And why is it you believe this person to be the missing Esther Hart, other than the lock of gray hair you, um, dislodged?"

"It's a very long story," Amanda said. "The longer we sit here gabbing, the more time the murderers have to make their escape." She jiggled her foot impatiently.

Finally relenting, the detective said, "I'll send a car out right away. You ladies are not to go anywhere. Is that clear?"

"Are we under arrest?" Marion said.

"No," said Detective Bright. "I just don't want to miss the rest of the 'very long story.' I'll be right back."

Amanda and Marion looked at each other. "Deep shit, my friend," Amanda said.

"We could make a run for it," Marion suggested. They both looked over at the door.

Amanda walked over and tried the doorknob. "The audacity!" she said. "It's locked. Does he think we'd try to escape?"

Marion sighed and shook her head.

A short while later, Detective Bright unlocked the door and stepped back into the room. He was met with two pairs of glaring eyes.

"You locked us in," Amanda said.

"Locks automatically," the detective replied. "Usually we interview criminals in here." He sat down across from the women and said, "From the beginning, please."

Marion and Amanda took turns laying out their story, beginning with signing up for the art class to, but not including, harboring Jeri Kay in their home. They skipped ahead to their discovery in the woods, interrupting each other to add details or correct timelines.

Detective Bright listened with no expression on his face and wrote in a small, spiral notebook.

When they'd finished, he said, "If your story—as unbelievable as it sounds—checks out, I'll be the first to say you two are amazing detectives. If not . . ." His eyebrows met in a "V" on his forehead.

"I know, I know," Marion interrupted. "We'll be fined for making a false report and escorted up to County Mental Health. Been there, done that." She sat back in her chair.

There was a knock on the door, and Detective Bright excused himself.

"Will they let us swing by the house and pick up some clothes before they send us to the nut house?" Amanda asked.

Moments later the detective reentered the room.

"It would appear . . ." he said, looking from one woman to the other, ". . . that part of your story checks out. There was a woman buried where you described. Pathology will have to check her DNA before we know for sure. Then her daughter will be notified to ID her and claim the body."

Amanda's shoulders dropped in relief. "What about the rest of our story?" she asked. "Did they find Jeri Kay and Marlene?"

"Jeri Kay?" The detective's eyebrows raised. "You know the identity of the other woman?"

Amanda flushed. A little knot of guilt at disclosing Jeri as an accomplice tightened in her stomach then released. "It's more of an educated guess, really," she mumbled.

"The officers found an encampment—a couple of tents and two guys living there. They said they hadn't seen any women."

"Oh, no! You were too late. I told you we were taking too much time," Amanda complained.

"Detective . . ." Marion leaned forward and met the detective eye to eye. "Those two men, although I'm sure they were highly credible . . ." Her words dripped with sarcasm. ". . . Were obviously lying. You're just going to have to take our word for it and put out an APB on the two women. They can't have gotten far. We're talking serial killers here."

"Not that I need you to tell me how to do my job," Detective Bright said with a hint of impatience, "but I would like you to work with our sketch artist to see if we can get some semblance of who we're looking for."

"Not necessary," Amanda said. "That happens to be my specialty. I used to work with the police, back in the day. And, besides, I can even put them in the clothes they were last seen wearing."

"She's really very good," Marion added.

Resigned, Detective Bright left to get a sketchpad. He returned and handed Amanda a large pad and her choice of charcoal or pencil. He turned to leave.

"Don't be locking the door," Amanda called out.

The detective cast a look back over his shoulder and mumbled something under his breath.

An hour later, Detective Bright appeared armed with a photographic-quality sketch of the two missing women and a detailed story that, while phantasmagorical in his considered opinion, seemed oddly congruent. The proper authorities were notified, and the search was official.

Back home, Amanda and Marion collapsed on the futon, kicked their shoes off, and slumped into fatigued silence.

Finally, Marion said, "We've done everything we can, yes?"

Amanda gave a slow nod.

"So, we can get on with our lives and leave this behind us, right?"

"I don't even know what 'getting on with our lives,' looks like anymore,'" Amanda said. "Dealing with bizarre events seems to have become our life."

"Maybe we need a reset," Marion suggested. "Like a vacation, somewhere entirely different to cleanse our mental pallets, as it were."

"A road trip?" Amanda said, rising to the suggestion.

Chapter Twelve

"North?" Marion shot a look of concern at Amanda as they drove in Amanda's VW Bug. "Just north? You mean we don't have a destination?"

Amanda, who had wholeheartedly embraced the idea of a road trip, had suggested they pack a suitcase with clothes enough for several days and a variety of weather conditions.

"Trust me, this will be fun," Amanda replied. "Haven't you always wanted to get in a car and go without any particular destination in mind?"

"Actually, I prefer to follow a map toward a place that I've carefully researched and have reservations."

"Well, today we're following our intuitions and mine says to go north." Amanda shot onto the Highway 101 on-ramp.

It was a sunny, clear, late-August morning in northern California. Amanda cranked her window down, and the smells of field grass, wildflowers, and country life infused the car. The breeze rippled her hair. She had a grin on her face and looked like a happy pixie.

Marion gave up trying to keep her hair from blowing in a tangle around her face. She grabbed Amanda's bedazzled baseball cap from the backseat, snugged it down on her head, and tried to relax into the adventure of it all.

"Here's a connector road." Amanda nodded at an exit sign ahead.

"What does it connect to?"

"No idea." She clicked on her turn signal and headed inland.

Well, there goes a day at the beach, Marion thought. Her mind drifted to another adventure Amanda had involved her in. It led them to Maui on a search for Amanda's long-lost lover, who eventually died of a drug overdose. Marion's face was grim with the memory of how that trip had turned out.

"You carsick?" Amanda asked. "You look kind of green."

"I was just thinking about Bonnie," Marion said. "You have odd taste in women."

Amanda cackled and turned on the radio to a 60's rock station.

And in music, Marion amended to herself.

"Oh, look. The Country General Store. We're just in time for lunch." Amanda pulled off the road into a small dirt parking area and killed the engine. "I'm famished."

Marion checked her watch. It was eleven o'clock.

"Good morning," Amanda called to the clerk as she made her way to the deli counter.

The dark-haired, bespeckled, clerk continued to lean against the back of his chair and stare straight ahead.

"Mmm, everything looks good," Amanda said. She rubbed her hands together excitedly. "What about you?"

"I'm not sure I've digested breakfast yet," Marion said. "Maybe I'll just have coffee. Sir?" She addressed the young man who continued to stare ahead.

"Well, that's weird," she whispered to Amanda. "Do you suppose he's on drugs?"

Amanda glanced over. "Maybe this is just a front for a wax museum," she said, her tone as hushed and intense as a conspiracy theorist. Her eyes sparkled with mischief. "I bet there's a hidden camera somewhere." She scanned the walls and ceiling of the small store. "C'mon. Let's have some fun."

Amanda walked behind the deli counter, looked pointedly at the clerk and said, "I think I'll just make myself a turkey sandwich to go." No response. "We just robbed a bank, you know. Worked up quite an appetite." Still nothing.

"Are you crazy?" Marion squeaked. "Whoever is filming us is probably calling the police at this very moment."

It occurred to her that she had just bought into Amanda's lunatic idea that this was a wax museum and the clerk wasn't real.

Marion took a deep breath, squared her shoulders, and walked over to the counter to confront the clerk. *Was he aware he could lose his job? He was apparently stoned out of his mind. Where was his boss? What was it with young people these days?*

"Young man," she demanded, leaning across the counter. Not only was he unresponsive, but his eyes were vacant, his lips blue-tinged, and there was no life-force energy.

"Oh, my God!" she screamed. "He's dead." She looked wildly at Amanda who continued to spread Mayo on her baguette. "We should do something. We should call someone," she said. Her voice verged on hysteria.

"We should probably leave. We were just cleared of one murder," Amanda said. She heaped sliced turkey on her sandwich, wrapped it in waxed paper, grabbed a handful of napkins, and walked over to Marion. "Yup, seems dead alright."

With shaking hands, Marion pulled her cell phone out of her purse.

"What are you doing?"

"I'm calling 9-1-1. We need help."

"Don't use your phone. They can trace it," Amanda said. She pointed to the wall phone behind the counter. "Here," she said, handing Marion a napkin. "Don't want to leave any prints."

Marion looked horror-stricken, but eased her way behind the counter, circumventing the dead young man. She lifted the landline receiver and punched in 9-1-1.

When the dispatcher answered, Marion said, "We're in The Country General Store. The young clerk appears to be dead. Please send help."

"What's your name please and your location?"

"I . . . um, I, well . . ." Marion's mind went blank. She had no idea where they were. She hung up the phone and said, "Let's get out of here."

They jumped in the car and sped out of the parking area leaving a cloud of dirt behind. Neither spoke for several miles. Every few minutes, Marion looked over her shoulder for any sign of the police.

"I can't believe we did that . . . just left that poor young man alone," Marion finally said.

"They'll find him. Nothing we could do. Can you imagine what would happen if we'd waited around? When the police came, they'd run our names through the system and tie us to the Jeri Kay mess. How would we explain all that?"

"I guess you're right. But, still . . ." Moments passed, and then Marion shook her head. "Things like this never happened to me before I met you."

"I'll take that as a compliment," Amanda said.

At random, she made a series of turns that eventually led them to an old highway bypass, going north again. Along the side of the road, a cardboard hand-lettered sign ahead read SPA.

"A spa? Right in the middle of nowhere?" Marion squinted as Amanda pulled up next to the sign and put the car in idle. There was no road, no driveway. They shrugged at one another, and Amanda continued up the road.

Around the next bend, another handmade sign said, Turn Here. There an overgrown dirt path with a hint of tire tread that suggested access—to where or what, they weren't sure. What they did know was the air smelled swampy. Marion wrinkled her nose.

"We can't possibly pass up an adventure like this, can we?" Amanda asked.

Marion knew that wasn't a question at all when Amanda turned onto the hint of the path and slowly followed it over a hill, through a stand of eucalyptus trees, and into a clearing. A redwood cottage. An outbuilding that sat back from the house.

In the parking area, several broken down pick-up trucks, a couple of road-worn RVs, and a tent camper stood side by side. "Must be a place only the locals know about," Marion said as she looked around.

They walked to the front porch. Like a reward for their faith and effort, a small sign on the door said, Welcome to Sulphur Spa.

"That would explain the smell," Marion said.

A small brass monkey served as a door knocker. Amanda lifted its little tail and let it slam back against the door. They heard footsteps approaching.

A gray-haired, sarong-draped, barefooted woman opened the door. "Welcome travelers. I am Grace. Here, you'll find peace." She guided them into a small reception room. A mixture of sage and incense filled the air. Indian bedspreads hung on the walls, and several meditation pillows were scattered about on the well-worn carpet. Candles cast a womblike glow all around the room. Burbling away in the corner sat a miniature waterfall and piped in music of bells chimed softly.

"All this, and I'm not even on acid," Amanda whispered to Marion.

Marion elbowed her.

"What may I offer you to soothe your weary souls?" Grace asked.

"What sort of services do you have?" Marion asked.

"The Great Spirit has provided us with land on which there are a natural mud bath and hot sulfur springs. My granddaughter, Brittney, is available to provide you with either a Reiki treatment or a hot-stone massage.

"Brittney?" Amanda mumbled under her breath.

"I noticed your parking lot was quite full. There are other guests?" Marion said.

"Those who need respite find us," Grace said. "Beyond this room, your outer-world clothes will not be necessary. We'll provide you with towels as needed."

Both women's eyebrows shot up, and they shared a momentary look of panic.

"Well, we've come this far," Amanda said.

They made the financial transaction and were taken to the bathhouse dressing room where they shed their "outer-world" clothes. Wrapped snuggly in oversized bath towels, Amanda and Marion warily made their way out back and down a flagstone path overgrown with moss. Guided by their noses as well as their vision, they found the mud bath—a large pond of hot, smelly mud in which several 'travelers' were blissfully immersed.

"They look happy as pigs," Amanda said quietly.

"I've never done this," Marion said. "You first." She motioned to Amanda.

Amanda looked around the pond and noted the towels strewn nearby on the grass. With more confidence than she was feeling, and with a when-in-Rome attitude, she tossed her towel aside and eased into the mud. Marion watched, wide-eyed.

"Oh, this is wonderful," Amanda said. She sank deeper and deeper until she appeared to be sitting on the bottom with only her neck and head free of mud. "Come on in."

"Shhh," someone said from across the pond.

"This is a silent area," someone else shared in a whisper.

Amanda nodded her an apology.

"I can't believe I'm doing this," Marion whispered. She dropped her towel, and with arms crossed over her breasts, pranced to the edge of the pond and lowered herself quickly into the hot mud.

"Ahh," she said. Several heads turned her way. "Sorry," she whispered.

They soaked neck deep in mud until their bodies released the tension. From time to time, a traveler would emerge from the muck like something from a horror movie. Dripping with stinking mud, they meandered along the path that led to the hot springs.

Finally, alone in the mud, they talked in undertones.

"I haven't felt this relaxed in . . . well, I can't even remember the last time," Marion said with a lazy smile.

"I feel like I don't a care in the world," Amanda said. She stretched her arms to the sky, and a plop of mud fell squarely on her head. "And now I've been baptized," she said with a chuckle.

Like a pair of Leviathans, they rose from the primordial ooze, wrapped themselves in their towels, and meandered down the path toward the hot springs. Only a handful of travelers remained.

Steam from the water hovered like fog—blurring details and lending certain anonymity to those bathing. She noticed two women sitting close together on a boulder on the far side of the water's edge.

Amanda cast her towel aside and dipped her toes in the water. She took a tentative step, then another, until she was knee deep. Mud slid off her body and floated away in the gentle burble of the springs.

She turned to Marion, who was still towel-clad, and whispered, "Toss me my towel, will you?" She waded in up to her waist as her body acclimated to the heat.

Marion tossed the mud-encrusted towel to Amanda and watched her make a quick laundry-agitation move on the submerged towel. She pulled it out, wrung it, and threw it onto the bank.

Preserving whatever modesty remained, Marion waded into the water, still fully wrapped, and only after complete submersion of her body, did she do a towel maneuver. She chuckled at her cleverness and tossed her towel onto the grass.

"The deeper you go, the hotter it seems to get," Marion observed quietly as she waded toward the center of the pond. She pulled her legs to her chest then stretched them out into a back float. Arching slightly, she tucked her chin to get better leverage and noticed her breasts looked like two overfilled water balloons bobbling on the surface. Gasping at the sight, Marion took in a mouthful of water, sputtered, coughed, flapped her arms about, and tried to right herself. Her legs pedaled spasmodically to find purchase in the mud.

"Marion!" Amanda shouted as she splashed her way deeper into the pond. She grabbed Marion by the arm and dragged her, still sputtering, to a shallow area near the boulder. As she glanced up, the two women who'd been there jumped up and scuttled off—not before the closeness in proximity revealed their identities.

Amanda clenched her teeth and refocused her attention on Marion who was now taking slow, deep breaths to calm herself after her ordeal.

"You saved my life," Marion said, grabbing Amanda's hand in gratitude.

"Yeah, yeah," Amanda said brusquely. "We've got to go." She tugged Marion out of the water and toward their towels.

"Wait . . . I'm sorry I made such a scene," Marion stammered as Amanda jogged them across the grass.

"Here," Amanda said. She threw one towel to Marion and the other over her shoulder. "Hurry or we'll lose them." She took off in the direction of the bathhouse.

"Lose who?" Perplexed, Marion followed at a brisk pace. When she reached the bathhouse, she found a dejected-looking Amanda slumped on a wooden bench. Her wet towel hung limply over her shoulder.

"They're gone. I knew it," Amanda said. "We were *that* close." She measured an inch with her fingers.

"Forgive me if I'm not following," Marion replied as she wrapped her towel around her and sat next to Amanda. "Who's gone?"

"Jeri and Marlene," Amanda said.

Chapter Thirteen

"What are the chances?" Amanda said, a day later. They sat in Amanda's kitchen at Marion's beautiful oak table. Her oak chairs had replaced Amanda's Salvation Army relics.

The introduction of Marion's furniture into Amanda's home had caused moments of tension, resolved by long conversations that wound up in compromise. Gone was the lumpy futon—replaced by a lovely couch with matching side chairs. Remaining was the steamer trunk that added just the right touch of bohemian to the room.

"What are the chances of stumbling upon Jeri Kay and Marlene out in the middle of nowhere?" Marion said.

"She must have thought she could throw us off by leaving my car at the airport. What did she take us for?"

"Everything she could, apparently," Marion said.

Over time, they'd developed a rhythm with one another, tuning in to the other's train of thought, picking up mid-conversation, and finishing each other's sentences. They were like an old married couple.

"I suppose we did the right thing by notifying Detective Bright. Maybe they can catch up with them—"

"Before they leave the state." Marion finished Amanda's sentence. "Well, we're back at square one. What's next?"

"Ziplining through the forest canopy? I've always wanted to try that," Amanda said.

"Why did you let me talk you into this?" Amanda huffed and puffed her way up yet another set of steps toward the first tower platform from which they'd begin their zip line experience.

"Perhaps you should have done some research before you booked our reservations," Marion said.

Amanda looked back over her shoulder—a drop of perhaps twenty feet—swooned and clung tightly to the guide ropes. "Good God," she mumbled.

Their guide, Marc, no more than a kid himself, waited on the platform above them, a big grin on his face. His eyes sparkled with mischief. "Just a few more yards," he called out. "You can do it."

Amanda pulled herself onto the platform and held onto the wood railing that partially boxed it in. "Oh, my God, my thighs are on fire. Tell me again . . . this is safe, right?"

"Perfectly safe," Marc said. "We've only lost three people this season." His expression was deadpan. "Nothing to worry about." Then a huge grin rearranged his face. "C'mon," he said. "You've already done the hardest part. Now just hang on and fly."

Marion finally reached the platform and squeezed in behind Amanda. She, too, grabbed the wood railing while catching her breath. "I can't believe we're doing this," she said to Amanda's back.

Amanda squirmed her way around and faced Marion. "You're always the calm one. You go first," she offered. 'If the cable doesn't snap, maybe I'll give it a try."

"No way," Marion said. "This was your nutty idea. You first. Who do you want to be notified, just in case?" she added.

Amanda shot her a look of contempt.

"Ladies, ladies," Marc chided. "Who will be the lucky one to begin the adventure of her lifetime? There can only be one 'first,'" he said. "Think of the stories you'll have to tell."

"Oh, okay," Amanda mumbled. She stepped forward and allowed Marc to harness her. He showed her how to use the thick gloves to slow herself down or speed up, according to how she placed her hands on the cable.

"You don't want to pull down too hard, or you'll stop mid-zip, and we'll have to send someone out to rescue you," he warned.

Terror flashed in Amanda's eyes.

"Look around, enjoy the view. There's nothing like it," Marc said. "Jose is on the next platform and will help you land safely. Remember, slow down as you approach." He checked her gear, secured her helmet, and hooked her onto the cable. "Ready?" he asked.

"Noooooo," Amanda hollered as she sailed off the platform and zipped the long stretch of cable above the trees, a deep valley, and a meandering creek.

"I'm going to *diiiieee*," she yelled, squinting her eyes. She pulled hard on the cable, and just as Marc had warned, she slowed to a stop a little more than mid-way between Platform 1 and Platform 2. She hung there, hyperventilating. "Help!" she hollered when she could catch her breath.

"Not to worry," Marc yelled back. "Jose is on his way out to get you. You'll be fine. Try to relax. Look around and enjoy the view," he suggested.

"Enjoy the view, my ass," she muttered. With nothing to do but wait to be rescued, she held her body as still as possible and ventured a peek below. A breathtaking view. A blue heron rested in the top boughs of a eucalyptus. Like molten lead, the creek snaked through the valley. The air was cool and fresh. A raven called from beyond the trees. Upriver, she saw a small campfire, white smoke curling into the sky. *It's the dry season. There's no camping this time of year*, she thought. *I should report this*.

Just as she began to relax her body, the cable jumped. She let out a scream and flailed her arms.

"It's okay. It's just me," Jose called as he worked his way toward Amanda. "You're safe. Just relax. I'm almost there."

Like a mantra, his voice soothed. Amanda settled back into her body.

Jose attached her halter to his own and worked his way back, hand over hand along the cable until they were both safe on Platform 2. He gave the thumbs up signal to Marc who made the final safety check on Marion's gear.

"Learn by example," he said. "Don't do that. Just let yourself glide." He gave Marion a little push, and off she went.

"Wheeeee!" Marion shouted as she hummed through the air. "Fantastic. I love it!" She took in the sights and sounds of the forest below. Slowing to a stop, Jose eased her onto the platform.

"This is the best idea you've ever had," she said to Amanda. She grabbed her in a clumsy hug. Amanda, pale and still shaken, seemed to hold onto Marion with a death grip.

The remaining four zips between platforms began pretty much the same as the first with Amanda hesitant but eventually making it all the way across. It wasn't until they were safely on the ground, unhooked from their gear, and headed back to their car that Amanda remembered the campfire sighting.

"On our way home," Amanda suggested, "let's follow the road that runs along the river. I saw a campfire from up above, and I just have a hunch—"

"That it's Jeri Kay and Marlene?" Marion finished. "Why would you think that?"

"Well, they can't have gotten very far, and camping out in the woods appears to be the kind of thing they do. I say we check it out."

They wound their way along the river, followed short trails off the road that ended in deserted campsites, and scanned the sky for signs of smoke.

After an hour, Marion said, "Okay, I'm over this. Call Detective Bright and tell him your suspicions. Maybe he can have a forest ranger do a more thorough check."

Amanda sighed in resignation, turned the car inland, and drove home.

"Could we agree to put the whole Jeri Kay thing behind us?" Marion asked as they entered the house. "Tracking down two middle-aged women is one thing, but a murderer and an accessory? I say we leave it in the hands of the police." She plunked herself down on the couch and took off her shoes.

Amanda stuffed her coat in the hall closet, mumbling her reluctant consent.

"I think I'll take a long, hot bath," Marion said. "That okay with you?"

"Yeah. I think I'd like chicken for dinner. I'll run to the market while you're in the tub." Amanda pulled her coat back out of the closet, grabbed her bag, and left.

About three blocks from home, Amanda's cell phone jangled. Figuring perhaps Marion had a couple more items she wanted from the market, Amanda pulled over to the curb and answered.

"I heard you," the voice said. "I saw you through my binoculars, you and Marion."

A bone-chilling shiver ran through Amanda.

"Jeri?" she said, her voice breaking.

"You've got to help me," Jeri said. "Marlene has gone completely off the deep end. I'm afraid she's going to kill me." She spoke rapidly and sounded scared. "Oh, no. She's back . . ." The line went dead.

Amanda immediately checked her call history and found Jeri's number. If she called back right now, it could put Jeri in danger. She'd wait and call later after talking with Marion. She knew Marion would discourage her from getting involved. Maybe she wouldn't tell Marion about the call . . .

Chapter Fourteen

"What's with you?" Marion lowered her reading glasses and looked at Amanda. "You've been fidgeting all night. You've got that frenetic energy. What aren't you telling me?"

They sat in the living room after dinner. Marion reading a novel and Amanda twisting her fingers and wiggling her feet while listening to NPR.

"I'm not *not* telling you anything," Amanda said too quickly. She glanced at Marion then away.

Marion narrowed her eyes and continued to stare at Amanda.

"Oh, okay," Amanda relented. "But you're not going to like it."

Marion raised her eyebrows, laid her book aside, and turned toward Amanda. "Spill it," she said.

"While I was driving to the market, Jeri called."

Marion grunted. "Go on."

"She said Marlene had 'lost it.' Jeri's afraid for her life. Before I could say anything, she hung up. I think Marlene must have walked in." She cast a pleading look at Marion. "We have to do something. I just don't know what. She could be in real danger."

"For heaven's sake, Amanda, so could we," Marion said, her voice strident. "The woman is nuts. You *know* she can't be trusted. We need to turn this over. You've got the phone number she called from?"

"Yes, but . . ." Amanda stalled. "Maybe I should talk with her first."

"What if you call and Marlene is standing next to her? She's not going to be able to talk to you."

"Um, I'll say I'm calling for a survey, and she can just say yes or no to my questions. She'd recognize my voice. I can ask if she's safe, if Marlene's nearby, if she can talk freely—stuff like that." Amanda began pacing the room.

"They're on the lam. Wouldn't Marlene think it odd that Jeri Kay would take time to answer a telephone survey?" Marion shook her head. "No, I don't think that's safe."

"How about if I just call and see if she answers? If not, I could leave a voicemail."

"You can't leave a voicemail!" Marion threw her hands in the air in exasperation. "What if Marlene listens to it? That could be the final straw of betrayal. She might just kill Jeri Kay on the spot. If there's Caller ID, she might come after *you*."

Amanda sat down on the couch. "Hadn't thought of that."

"You're still thinking with your heart, not your head," Marion said.

With a sigh of resignation, Amanda said, "Okay, we'll call Detective Bright first thing in the morning."

"I'm glad you've finally come to your senses." Marion reached over and patted Amanda's knee. "I think I'll turn in now. Don't stay up too late—we need to be clear-headed for this conversation tomorrow."

"Right. I just want to catch the rest of this NPR program." She curled up next to the radio and turned the volume up a notch. "G'night."

Somewhat later, Amanda checked for light under Marion's door. Finding none, she slipped her coat on, tucked her cell phone into her pocket, and quietly let herself out the kitchen door. She carefully navigated the backyard, lit only by a sliver of moon. When she reached the fence, she pulled out her phone and, after taking a deep, slow breath, dialed the last number on her call log.

The phone rang three times, and then someone picked up, but said nothing.

Amanda debated whether she should speak or wait out the silence. *What if it was Marlene on the other end of the line? If it was Jeri, why wouldn't she speak? Oh, no . . . the Caller ID thing—I forgot about that. I have to say something.*

"Hello? I'm calling for Maude Harper. Is this the right number?" Maybe Jeri would recognize her voice and speak if she could. If it was Marlene, she'd just thrown her off track.

Click. Whoever answered hung up. "Damn," Amanda muttered in despair.

The next morning, Detective Bright sat in the side chair across from their couch. Hair slicked in place, he smelled of dry cleaning solvent. He wore pleated pants, and his shoes were polished.

Amanda and Marion sat on the edge of the couch cushion like two schoolgirls called into the principal's office.

"How long have you had this 'new information' you're about to share?" he asked, leaning forward.

"I told you we should have called right away," Marion said out of the side of her mouth to Amanda. "Now we're in trouble."

"Not really all that long," Amanda hedged. "Is that important?"

"It may be. Ms. Dowdy has already been remanded into custody."

Both women sighed in relief.

"That's great, right?" Amanda said.

"I know this has been an unorthodox experience for you, Detective Bright, but could you give us any more facts?" Marion asked. "Not knowing the outcome has been so stressful."

"She confessed to the murder of Mrs. Hart but pled innocent of any other murders. The other woman has not yet been apprehended." He addressed Amanda. "Might you have any information on her whereabouts?"

Amanda's eyes widened. "Not really, no." She shook her head. *Thank God, she's safe from harm*, Amanda thought. Her next thought—*that must have been Jeri on the phone*. "I mean, there was a call from her a week or so ago, but we didn't actually speak."

Marion cleared her throat and looked at her hands folded in her lap.

"How did you know it was her?" Detective Bright asked. He shifted his position and seemed somehow larger. Amanda squirmed.

"My phone log," she said.

"I'll need that number." He waited without speaking while Amanda retrieved her cell phone and reluctantly gave him the number.

"If you hear from her again, I'll need to know," the detective said. His expressionless face belied his accusatory tone. "It appears she has a history of psychiatric illness, and was, according to Ms. Dowdy, responsible for a series of unsolved murders across the United States. She's considered armed and extremely dangerous."

Amanda's jaw dropped.

Marion gasped and slapped her hand over her heart. After she'd regained her composure, she said, "I'm not sure Ms. Dowdy would be the most credible person to be pointing fingers."

Detective Bright narrowed his eyes at her. "Our Government people are all over this case. We're following any leads." He turned again to Amanda. "You will let us know if she tries to contact you." It wasn't a request.

Amanda nodded.

"Do not try to contact her. Let the police handle it from here on," the detective warned.

After they'd seen the detective to the door, Marion spun around and confronted Amanda.

"You lied! You didn't tell him about the campfire, or the call when she suddenly hung up. Oh,

Amanda, what were you thinking?" Visions of the FBI bashing in their door and hauling them off to interrogate them swam in her head.

"This is obstruction of justice." Marion clamped both hands on top of her head as if to keep it from exploding. "Armed and dangerous? She's a serial killer. Oh, my God, we are *so* doomed," she cried.

"I didn't lie about not knowing where she was," Amanda said in a small voice. *And what if she did know where Jeri was? What if Marlene was telling the truth? What if Jeri was certifiably crazy and dangerous?*

She curled up on the end of the couch facing away from Marion's accusations and turned on NPR. She turned the volume up to drown out the niggling awareness that Jeri had said she was afraid for her life, that Marlene had lost touch with reality . . .yet Marlene was already in custody.

She'd lied.

Chapter Fifteen

Days turned into weeks with no word from Jeri Kay. Life resumed its humdrum routine, except the addition of a seniors' yoga class—Marion's idea.

"Namaste," the instructor said, bowing to her students as she ended the class.

"This is ridiculous," Amanda muttered as she rolled up her mat. "I'm too old and too fat to turn myself into a pretzel."

"Were both a little out of shape is all. We'll get there," Marion encouraged. "Besides, the only other class that wasn't full was Zumba." She smirked at the thought.

As they put on their shoes, Amanda's cell phone buzzed in her bag. She reached for it, and then quickly withdrew her hand. If it was Jeri, she couldn't talk right now.

"You don't usually get calls," Marion mused. "Should you maybe check it?"

"Probably just someone wanting to sell me something or donate to a cause. I'll check it later."

"Maybe the NRA wants you to renew your membership." They chuckled.

Autumn was in the air. The women drove home with the windows down and breathed in the warm, pungent smell of September.

"I think I'll rake the backyard. I feel like doing something autumny," Marion said as they pulled into the driveway.

"Hey, knock yourself out," Amanda said. "I'm going to finish that mystery novel. I think I know how it ends, but I want to make sure I'm right."

She pulled the book out of her bag, along with her cell phone. Acting as though it was an afterthought, she checked the "calls missed." The familiar number swam before her eyes. She scratched her head as if bugs were crawling on her scalp. "Damn, damn, damn," she said quietly. The longer Amanda stared at the phone, the more light-headed she became.

At least the threat of Marlene answering was no longer a factor. And Marion would be busy in the yard for hours. With her heart pounding, she pushed "return call."

The phone rang five times. Just as she was about to hang up, someone answered, but again, no one spoke. Amanda decided she'd wait it out. After a few seconds, the tension got to her, and she said, "Jeri, is that you?"

"Oh, God, Amanda, is that you?" Jeri sounded breathless.

Ridiculous as it seemed, a warmth spread down the length of Amanda's body, and she sighed with relief.

"I didn't know if I'd hear from you again. Are you okay? Where are you?" Amanda's words came tumbling out.

"I've been on the run. Everywhere I go, Marlene finds me. Then she stalks me, biding her time."

"*Liar, liar, pants on fire,*" Amanda thought.

Amanda, I know she's going to kill me. This cat-and-mouse game is torture. You've got to help me escape. *Please*. You're the only one I can count on, the only one I trust."

Amanda's blood ran cold. Certifiably crazy. Delusional. Paranoid. Dangerous. Psychopath. The words rattled around in her head.

"Jeri, I want to help you." *Did that sound like I'm on to her? No*, she reassured herself. *That would have been*, '*Jeri, you need help*!'

"Where are you now? Where can we meet?" Amanda said, keeping her voice even.

"I'm in Las Vegas."

"Las Vegas?" Amanda shook her head. "Why are you in Vegas?"

"It's easier to blend into the crowd here," Jeri said, sounding sane and reasonable.

"Okay . . ." Amanda said, stalling. Unsure of where to go from there, she said, "How can I help you? What do you need?"

"I need a safe place to stay. Can you come get me?"

Amanda smacked her forehead. "Gee, Jeri, I don't trust my Bug to make it that far. Where are you staying in Vegas?"

"Why?" Jeri said, sounding suddenly suspicious. "If you're not going to come get me, why do you need to know where I'm staying?"

Caught off-guard, Amanda winged it. "I'm concerned about your safety." She listened to the silence. "Is there any way you can get back here to California? We could meet up."

"I suppose I could pick up another car," Jeri said, still sounding guarded.

Amanda didn't want to think about what would be involved in "picking up another car." A car-jacking, maybe? Some little old lady slaughtered and left in a ditch, car and purse missing?

"What happened to your car?" Amanda knew she was pushing it and kept her voice conversational. "Hope it didn't break down on you. Do you have AAA, by the way?"

There was an irritable huff, followed by, "I left it in New Mexico when Marlene caught up with me. I had to run for my life. So, are you going to help me, or what?" Her voice had a hostile edge now.

It made Amanda's skin crawl, but she knew what she had to do next.

"If you can get back over the state line, I'll meet you anywhere you want. You can stay with me. I'll keep you safe. Marlene will never find you." At least the last part was true—unless they wound up in the same prison.

"I don't know. Maybe." The line went dead.

A shiver of dread shook Amanda from head to toe.

The back door slammed, and Amanda jumped.

Marion stomped her feet on the mat, no doubt freeing her shoes of autumnal detritus. A little bit of ordinary was just what Amanda needed.

"So, were you right?" Marion said, all chipper from her workout.

Wide-eyed with guilt, Amanda said, "Right about what?" She'd been right, all right. Jeri was a walking psychiatric diagnosis—several of them perhaps.

"The end of the mystery? Did you get it right?"

Amanda felt she was having two different conversations using the same words.

"Um, I'm not sure. I think so. I haven't quite finished it yet.

Chapter Sixteen

Two weeks had passed, and still no contact from Jeri. Amanda kept her phone with her at all times. The plan was to secure a meeting place and then let Detective Bright know. He would make sure the proper police presence was there to arrest Jeri as soon as Amanda laid eyes on her.

She'd never betrayed a friend before. Then again, Jeri wasn't actually a friend. She was a demented psychopath who probably wouldn't show up anyway. Another mark on Amanda's credibility.

Was keeping this to herself betraying Marion? Amanda didn't want to think about that. *It was just easier with fewer people in the mix*, she reasoned. She glanced out the living room window. The overcast day was melting into evening.

Why hadn't Jeri called?

"Dinner," Marion called. It was her night to cook. Baked halibut, steamed kale, and pickled beets were on the menu. Two ramekins of *flan* sat on the counter for dessert.

"Smells great," Amanda said. She rubbed her hands together in anticipation. "What's this?" she said, picking up a brochure that was sitting on the table. "Serenity Tours?" She opened it to see a crowd of smiling seniors aboard a cruise ship. "Should be called Senility Tours by the looks of it," she mused.

"I think we should consider a cruise," Marion said. "We haven't done anything fun in ages."

"Gee, we're doing yoga every week. That's great fun."

"Don't be snarky. I know you don't like yoga. Have you ever been on a cruise ship?"

"Nope."

"Look at all the activities. And the food!"

"What's fun about a big boat carrying a group of seasick seniors?" Amanda opened the brochure.

"They have medicine for that."

"Where would we go?"

"I'm thinking Mexico," Marion said with a grin.

Amanda's first thought—*what if Jeri called*? *How would I get to her*? Followed by, *can you get cell reception aboard a ship*?

"Why is your brow wrinkled? Are you concerned about the food or water? We'd mostly be eating onboard. It's perfectly safe, you know," Marion prattled on.

"It sounds fine," Amanda said. She'd have to come up with a Plan B. "Let's do it."

After dinner, Marion occupied herself making reservations and gathering all the information they would need for their three-day cruise.

"You'll probably want to get a new swimsuit," Marion suggested.

"What's wrong with my current swimming apparel?"

"Men's boxer shorts and a sleeveless T-shirt are fine for the ocean," Marion reasoned, "but maybe not so much for poolside."

Amanda sighed.

"Oh, and dinner wear; we'll need something fancy for evenings."

"Are you trying to talk me out of this?"

"Oh, come on. It will be fun. We'll go shopping this weekend." Marion added more items to her long list of pre-vacation tasks. "I'm so excited."

Amanda rolled her eyes.

The next morning after breakfast, Marion said, "Sears has a sale on summer wear. Shall we check it out?"

As Amanda loaded the dishwasher, she said over her shoulder, "Would you check it out for us? I'm not much in the shopping mood. If you see something you think I can't live without, just pick it up for me. Okay?"

"Really?" Marion's eyes lit up. "You'd let me do that?"

"I think it's the lesser of two evils," Amanda muttered.

"Someone got up on the wrong side of the bed this morning," Marion said as she left the kitchen.

Without Marion chirping about the house, Amanda sunk into a funk she'd felt coming on for days. She paced the living room, unsure why the feelings of gloom and doom were so pervasive, almost palpable.

Her cell phone rang. An image of Jeri shot through her mind. Or had the image flashed just before the phone rang? Either way, she glanced at the Caller ID and nearly dropped the phone. It was Jeri.

Amanda broke out in a sweat. Her voice cracked as she said, "Hello?"

Silence.

"Jeri, I know this is you. Please, talk to me. I've been so worried about you."

"I feel so safe hearing your voice," Jeri said. "I'm back in California like you suggested. You've got to help me. I think I saw Marlene in a casino just before I left. If she's followed me here, she'll kill me."

"I'll do whatever I can, Jeri." Amanda focused all the sincerity she could muster up in her voice. "Where are you? Let me come get you. I'll keep you safe." She cringed at such a blatant lie.

"I'm thinking of going to Canada. Will you come with me?"

"Um, uh . . ." Amanda knew if she didn't go along with this, she'd lose track of Jeri for sure. She was so close; she couldn't botch it now.

"I have to put some things in order first," she said. "Can you meet me somewhere near here? If you want, we can even take my car so Marlene won't be able to track you." *Okay, that sounded convincing.* Then she remembered telling Jeri she didn't think her Bug could make it as far as Vegas. *Do crazy people remember details like that?*

They agreed to meet at a Park-and-Ride lot on the outskirts of town in one week, at noon. They could abandon Jeri's car there.

"We're going to have a wonderful life together, Amanda," Jeri said, her voice breathy with promise. "You just wait and see."

"I can't wait," Amanda said.

As soon as they'd hung up, Amanda dropped to the couch. Her head swam, and nausea threatened to dislodge her breakfast. She took several shaky breaths, checked her call log, and dialed Detective Bright before she lost her courage.

"Ms. Pritchard, you've done the right thing," the detective said with a hint of amazement in his voice. He reviewed the details one more time and promised the proper authorities would be in place. All she had to do was get out of her car and wait for Jeri Kay to walk towards her. They would take it from there.

"What will happen to her?" Amanda couldn't help the tug she felt at her heart. After all, the poor woman was sick.

"She'll be evaluated at the psychiatric facility. They'll determine if she can stand trial. Either long-term hospitalization for the criminally insane or prison will be her future. You're doing the right thing, you know," the detective reassured her. This time he sounded as though he meant it.

Emotionally spent, Amanda dragged a lawn chair into a patch of sun in the backyard. She felt the weight of her decision.

Should she tell Marion?

The sound of Marion calling to her from the kitchen window created a moment of disorientation as Amanda's eyes popped open. She looked at her watch. "Must have fallen asleep," she muttered.

"Come see what I got. You're going to love it!" Marion's voice sparkled with excitement.

Amanda wiped a trickle of drool from her chin and ambled into the house.

In the living room, Marion sat on the couch and grinned like a four-year-old at Christmas. She was surrounded by shopping bags with a colorful array of beachwear, sun hats, and what Amanda imagined would be their dinner wear.

Marion kept a running monolog as she showed each piece to Amanda. "Who knew shopping could be so much fun," she said. "What did you do this afternoon?"

"Oh . . ." Amanda hesitated, "I guess I fell asleep in the backyard."

Decision made.

Chapter Seventeen

"Where the hell is my wallet?" Amanda said. She tossed the pillow across the couch, shoved a book aside, picked up the cat and looked.

"I imagine it's where you left it last night, on the kitchen table." Marion narrowed her eyes and asked, "Everything okay? You seem a little cranky this morning."

"Fine. Just fine. My keys . . ."

"On top of the TV. What would you do without me?" Marion teased.

Amanda turned toward Marion, opened her mouth as if to say something, thought better of it, and closed her mouth.

"I have a bunch of errands to run. Back in a couple of hours. Need anything while I'm out?" Amanda grabbed her keys and headed for the door.

"No. Have fun. See you later."

Feeling like an adolescent who lied to her mother to sneak out to meet an illicit lover, Amanda plodded to her car with stooped shoulders. She felt burdened by the heaviness of what she was about to do. Her hand shook as she reached for the door handle. "Good God, what have I gotten myself into?" she said under her breath. *Geez, I could die doing this.* She sat behind the wheel and put two fingers to her carotid artery. Her pulse raced. She took several long, deep breaths then started the engine.

Amanda arrived at the Park-and-Ride twenty minutes early. She pulled into a spot farthest from any other cars and turned off the engine. Looking around, she saw no one. Her mind went into overdrive. *What if there's no backup? What would she do about Jeri? Detective Bright told her they'd be out of sight. But what if plans changed? What if the police were at the wrong Park-and-Ride? What if they arrive too late? What choice would she have then? Take a drive with Jeri?* She checked her cell phone. No messages. *What if Jeri didn't show up?*

"Stop it, you're making yourself crazy." She thrummed her fingers on the steering wheel then checked the backseat where she usually kept a couple of paperbacks.

She grabbed a collection of lesbian erotica by Radclyffe. That should take her mind off things. Just as she opened the book, an undercover cop car—she could spot them—drove slowly through the Park-and-Ride. The driver didn't make eye contact, just kept on going, right out the exit. "Hmm," she said and rechecked her watch. Five minutes until noon. She closed the book. Too unfocused to read, she sat back in her seat.

A dusty blue Volvo pulled in, hesitated just beyond the entrance, and then parked five cars down from Amanda's car. The windows were tinted, and she couldn't make out the driver. No one exited the vehicle. "Oh, yeah," Amanda reminded herself. "I'm supposed to get out and stand by my car."

Jo Lauer

Amanda took a deep breath, opened the door, stood, and stretched. Then she leaned against the back of her VW, legs crossed at the ankles, casual. She glanced at the Volvo, and then scanned the parking lot. *No one. Not even the unmarked. Shit.* She heard the creak of a door opening slowly.

Jeri emerged from the Volvo. She checked the lot before reaching into her backseat for a large tote. She acknowledged Amanda only by a nod of her head. She closed her car door, and squinting against the sun, she turned toward Amanda. A smile brightened her face. Jeri threw her tote over her shoulder and began crossing the lot.

Amanda uncrossed her ankles, took a step forward, and broke into a sweat. Her knees threatened to give way. *Jeri was no more than nine yards away. For God's sake, where were the police? Six yards away. Jeri was reaching into her tote. Did Jeri have a gun?* Four yards . . . *Is this how I'm going to die?*

Out of nowhere appeared two unmarked, Sheriffs' cars, a wagon, three HPs, and several other backup cars, probably Feds. The entrance and exit were suddenly blocked, and men with guns drawn jumped from their vehicles and descended on Jeri, who stood openmouthed and rigid.

As they approached her, she snapped, spun wildly, screamed like a banshee on fire, fought with flailing arms and feet, and spat profanities.

Amanda cowered, covered her ears, and stared at the ground. Tears stung her eyes.

Once Jeri was restrained, Amanda risked a glance and was met with an icy glare of betrayal and hatred. She quickly turned her head away as the cops dragged Jeri to a waiting vehicle.

Amanda slumped against the back of her car and fought off an urge to vomit. Cars began to disperse. One of the backups pulled next to her, and Detective Bright emerged.

"It's over," he said. "You okay?" He unscrewed the top of a water bottle and handed it to Amanda.

Amanda's shook with uncontrollable spasms. The detective put a beefy hand on her shoulder to steady her.

"You're going to be okay. It's just energy passing through. You did good." They stood together in the lot.

When her circuitry had calmed down, and she'd had some water, she asked, "Is it really over?"

"It's as over as it gets," he said, with something close to a smile. "Thanks to you."

Detective Bright got into his car and drove away.

Once home, Amanda sat in her car. How was she going to explain the last week to Marion? She considered saying she'd heard from Detective Bright—Jeri had been apprehended, and their worries were over.

As she pondered, Marion came from around back pulling the recycle bin to the curb. She waved at Amanda then came over and stood next to the car.

She tapped on the window, and Amanda rolled it down.

"What on earth are you doing sitting in the car with the windows up? It's hot outside."

Amanda blinked and shrugged.

"Oh, my . . . you don't look so good," Marion said. "What's wrong? Come on, come inside." She opened the driver's door and took Amanda's clammy hand. "Are you getting that flu that's going around? Maybe it's heatstroke. Do we need to get you to the doctor?" she asked as she supported a wobbly Amanda into the house.

As soon as Amanda collapsed onto the couch, she burst into tears. Marion sat next to her and wrapped her arms tightly around her sobbing roommate. "There, there," she crooned. "Whatever it is, it's going to be all right."

"God, you must have a cramped neck holding me like this," Amanda said as her sobs subsided.

"I'm fine." Marion rolled her shoulders and stretched her neck. "Do you think you can tell me what happened?"

Amanda backtracked to last week's phone call from Jeri. In chronological order, she laid out the steps that led to her current emotional collapse.

Marion listened, speechless, her mouth agape. She shook her head slowly. "Oh, my God, you poor thing. Why did you think you had to do this all by yourself?" she asked when Amanda finished her story. "That was so dangerous. You could have . . ." her voice trailed off.

"If Jeri had known you were involved, she'd have never agreed to meet. And," Amanda hung her head, "I thought you'd get in the way and blow up the plan." She peered up at Marion expecting to see anger.

Tears brimmed in Marion's eyes. "You're right. I probably would have." She gave a sad smile. "Are we okay?" She took Amanda's hand in both of hers.

Amanda nodded, then gave her a hug and hung on tight. "Now we can go on our cruise without me being obsessed about whether or not Jeri would call," she said into Marion's shoulder.

They made a pact to turn their cell phones off in celebration of being free of the entire Jeri Kay business.

"It's all in the past," Marion said, patting Amanda's back. "Fresh start, agreed?"

Amanda nodded.

Chapter Eighteen

Three weeks into their fresh start, Amanda and Marion flew from SFO to Long Beach. A shuttle took them to the docking area where they boarded their ship.

"Damn, this is big," Amanda said, eyes wide in amazement. "It's like a floating city."

They followed the crowd up the gangplank into a receiving area where they handed photo IDs—to be scanned each time they boarded or left the ship—received key cards to their stateroom, and their luggage was tagged to be delivered later.

Again, they trailed behind passengers who seemed to know where they were going and arrived at a bank of elevators. Amanda checked her key card. "Level 3," she said and grabbed onto Marion's sleeve as they entered the elevator. She wrinkled her nose. "It smells like someone threw up in here," she whispered to Marion. "Did you remember the motion-sickness pills?"

"Will you relax? You're bringing me down." Marion's impatience was building. "This is an adventure. It's supposed to be fun." She shook her sleeve loose from Amanda's grasp.

Their stateroom was neat and tidy, but small. It reminded Amanda of navigating her kitchen at home.

Before launching, they met in various stations for orientation. In the lifeboat area, the staff person said, "When you hear this sound," he paused while a loud horn blast made Marion jump. "Go immediately to one of the muster stations in case of evacuation."

"Evacuation?" Amanda gulped. "In the middle of the ocean?" She clamped her hands solidly on the railing.

Marion patted her on the back. "We're never really all that far from shore," she whispered. She didn't know if that was true, but she saw Amanda was getting herself all wound up.

"Did you forget I don't know how to swim'" Amanda said.

"Ah right," Marion said, her voice softening.

Their group flocked to the main deck across from the dock. "Where are all the throngs of people with signs, balloons, and confetti, screaming bon voyage and waving like maniacs?" Amanda asked. "There's just a few stray people looking at the big ship. But no send-off. No streamers. Well, that's a major letdown," she grumbled, immediately regretting her remark.

Following another loud blast from a horn, the ship began a very subtle movement forward out of its berth.

"Is that all there is?" Amanda relaxed her shoulders. She looked at Marion who had her face turned to the afternoon sun and was breathing in the salty sea air.

They took a walk around the deck, checked out the amenities—several pools, an abundance of restaurants and bars, a couple of casinos, and several dance floors—then went back to their stateroom to rest up for dinner.

"I can't feel us moving. Are you sure we're going anywhere? What if we're stuck?" Amanda paced the tiny room.

"Oh, for God's sake," Marion said. "Look out the porthole."

"All I see is water," Amanda complained. "Oh, wait . . . We're away from the shore. That's good, right?"

"Amanda, you've got to relax. I know you've been through a harrowing experience, but it's over now. No more bad things are going to happen. You're safe; you're on vacation . . ." Marion's voice took on a hypnotic quality. "Breathe in. Breathe out. All is well."

"You're right. I'm being ridiculous. Okay. Fresh start," Amanda said.

When they'd dressed for dinner, Marion nodded. "You clean up nicely."

Amanda beamed. Marion had bought her an off-white linen pantsuit and a splashy purple and lavender scarf. Amanda gave herself the once-over in the mirror on the back of the bathroom door. "Not bad for an old broad," she agreed.

Marion twirled in her sea-green dress with a full skirt. She seemed to look and feel younger and more vibrant than Amanda had seen in quite some time.

"Nice," Amanda said with a smile.

As they approached the dining area, Amanda took Marion's arm to steady herself and quell her own panic of being among people who knew how to behave in social situations.

Marion glanced at her. "Well, if we're going to do this . . . let's at least do it right." She interlocked her arm with Amanda's. "I would most likely be the femme, right?"

They bumped elbows as they awkwardly reconnected. Marion took Amanda's arm, and they walked into a dining room resplendent with white linen tablecloths and silver tableware. Crystal flutes and wine glasses sparkled on the tables. There was no assigned seating, so they made their way to an unoccupied table.

Cocktails. Skipped the appetizers. On to salad.

"Start with the fork on the outside," Marion whispered.

With Marion's guidance, Amanda's shoulders relaxed.

Marion ordered a seafood platter and a glass of Chardonnay. Amanda chose steak—rare, just beyond mooing—with a California Shiraz. Desserts, passed on a tray, were works of art as well as sumptuous. After finishing a chocolate Grenache torte, Amanda glanced at Marion as the dessert tray came around again. Marion gave a discreet nod, and Amanda helped herself to a slice of lemon meringue pie. She grinned like a child at a birthday party.

"This is the life, huh?" Amanda said between bites. "I don't know why we didn't do this sooner."

Marion couldn't help but laugh.

On their return trip to their room, they passed several nightclubs with music blaring. Party-people drank, danced, and shouted to hear each other. They exchanged glances, smiled, shook their heads, and continued on to their room.

"Oh, look at that!" Amanda exclaimed. "Our covers have been turned down. I can't remember the last time someone turned down the blankets." Her voice sounded sad as she stood staring at her bed, nostalgic for something she'd never had.

Marion stopped, glanced at Amanda, and gave her a gentle smile.

As they changed into their nightclothes and crawled into their separate beds, Marion said, "You know, we've never really talked about where we come from." She looked at Amanda who was fluffing her pillow.

"I was raised by wolves," Amanda said.

Marion startled.

"Not literally, of course. But my parents were backwoods people from the Ozarks who migrated to California when I was little. They never quite figured out how to 'do society.'" Amanda laughed. "Explains a lot, right?"

Marion, quiet, simply nodded.

"I learned by watching other people." Amanda continued.

"You've done an amazing job," Marion replied.

"I got stuck in the hippie era—you may have noticed," Amanda confessed with a quirky smile. "It was a relief to finally be accepted. Ah, those were the good old days—bright tie-dyed clothes, organic food, and good drugs." She chuckled to herself. "I lived in a commune for a while. Then I traded it all to get married. I would have followed him anywhere. He had charisma going for him, but that's about all."

Marion shuddered.

"Easy, Marion! Not Jim-Jones charisma." Amanda rolled her eyes. "What about you?" She snuggled down under her covers.

"Oh, nothing so interesting, I'm afraid." She yawned and rolled over onto her back. "Both my parents were teachers—"

"That's why you speak so good," Amanda interrupted.

"*Well*," Marion corrected automatically. "Their friends were all academic-types. We were expected to grow up, go to college, get married, and live the next generation of our parents' lives."

"How did you escape?" Amanda's turned onto her side to face Marion.

"I almost didn't. I did the college thing and even married. Her voice turned bitter. But, I picked a cad who cheated on me with someone young enough to be our child, which we never had." She turned her head to look at Amanda whose eyes were closed and mouth was open in a gentle snore.

"Told you it was boring," she said. She reached over and turned out the bedside light.

Chapter Nineteen

The next morning, the cruise ship docked among old creaking piers along the shore of Ensenada, Mexico. After breakfast onboard, Amanda and Marion disembarked and took a tour bus into town.

The bus passed a smattering of low-level houses and buildings that sat in front of gently rolling hills. When they climbed off the vehicle, the two adventurers emptied into a noisy, chaotic, and colorful marketplace filled with souvenir stalls and restaurants—all kept in business by the tourist trade.

Dust puffed up with each footstep as they strolled along the path. They passed an array of merchandise and stopped at a stall where a woman hawked intricate silver necklaces interlaced with small turquoise stones. Marion examined one with an appreciation for its artistry. The saleswoman's insistence that they buy a necklace propelled the women on down the lane.

"I will not be bullied into buying something just because I'm a tourist," Amanda said.

They moved on, now aware that they should keep a safe distance.

Barefooted children kicking up dust, swarmed the tourists, hawking everything from packages of gum to hand-beaded bracelets.

Colorful handwoven blankets flapped in the breeze. Amanda was drawn to one with subtle earth tones. She smiled as she ran her fingers over the weave. "Beautiful," she said to the young woman sitting at a loom, surrounded by colorful yarn.

"Gracias." The woman smiled and nodded.

"How much?" Amanda asked.

"$25," the woman said, a question in her voice.

"Oh, no . . ." Amanda gasped. At home she would have paid up to $200 for a blanket like this.

"Sorry," the woman said, ducking her head. "I'll give it to you for $20."

"No, no . . . that's not what I meant." Amanda stumbled over her words. The last thing she wanted was to devalue a third-world woman struggling to make a living.

"Final offer, $15." The woman shoved the blanket at Amanda.

Stunned, Amanda blinked. She withdrew $50 from her purse, handed it to the woman, and took the blanket.

Dazed, Amanda turned to look for Marion who was surrounded by a gaggle of children. She motioned to Marion.

"What was going on over there?" Marion asked. "You look pale. Are you okay?"

"Hungry," Amanda replied. "I think I worked up an appetite haggling over the price for a hand-woven blanket. I'd give anything for a fish taco."

"We passed a taco shop just a block or so back. Let's go," Marion replied, turning back the way they had come.

"Please, *Señoras*," said a man standing nearby. "Don't eat there."

Both Amanda and Marion looked at the man suspiciously.

He was handsome, near their age, with steel-gray hair, and a matching mustache. Dressed in a business suit, his shoes were polished to a reflective shine—even in the midst of the dusty street. He seemed out of place in this casual tourist-laden burg.

"Sorry to have overheard," he apologized. "But for the best, most authentic fish taco, you must follow me."

Both Amanda and Marion took a reflexive step back.

"I've heard stories about tourists who vanish this way," Amanda stage-whispered to Marion.

"Thank you, but—" Marion began.

"Ah, you are right to be concerned. You are two beautiful women in a foreign land, and a strange man tries to lure you away from the crowd. I apologize." His smile was warm, genuine.

Amanda softened a bit and returned his smile.

"Remember, you were a sucker once for charisma, and it didn't turn out well," Marion said to her.

"I want only for you to have the best experience of my homeland. I will tell you how to get there." He directed them down the street, left, then right, then left. He described various landmarks to help them find their way. "*Buenos Dias*," he said, bowing from the waist.

"What the hell," Amanda said. "When in Rome, or Mexico . . ." They followed the man's directions and rounded a corner. There stood a small shack with a hand-lettered wooden sign that read, Ensenada Tacos. They ate at a wooden picnic table under the filtered shade of a scrawny tree. Small black birds pecked at the ground near their feet.

Amanda patted her stomach. "Mystery man knows what he's talking about. I've never had a fish taco this good." She took a swig of warm beer from her bottle.

"This is turning out to be quite the adventure, isn't it," Marion said with a lazy smile. "Taking a cruise, haggling prices, eating tacos on a beach in Mexico . . . and being called beautiful." She wiped her mouth with a tissue from her bag, sat back, and peeked at her watch. "Time to wander back to the ship. Wouldn't want them to leave without us," she said.

They followed their directions in reverse, but the road they'd begun from seemed to have disappeared.

"Oh, no. Where are we?" Amanda fretted. "Nothing looks familiar."

"We must have made a wrong turn. Let's go back to the taco place and try again." Marion glanced at her watch, took a deep breath, and tried not to panic. *Surely, they wouldn't leave without everyone on board . . . Would they?*

They started down a dusty street but took a shortcut to the right when a barking pit bull, fangs bared, blocked their way.

"Maybe we should knock on someone's door and ask directions," Amanda suggested.

"May I remind you we're in Mexico, and neither of us speaks Spanish." They walked on, craning their necks for anything that looked familiar.

A small child, maybe four years old, was standing in the street in front of a house. He stirred the dirt with a long stick. Marion put on her best friendly teacher face and said, "Hello. Do you speak English?"

The boy's eyes grew wide and then filled with tears. He turned and ran into his house.

"Oh, dear," Marion said.

Moments later, a woman, perhaps the child's mother, appeared at the door. She stared at them. The boy peeked out from behind her.

"Go on, give it another try," Amanda said, urging Marion forward.

This time Marion resorted to universal gestures. She smiled. She pointed to herself and Amanda. She looked to the right then the left and shrugged. She held her hands out in a plea for help.

The woman stepped away from the door and walked closer to them.

Marion pantomimed the waves on the ocean and a large boat. She held her head and made a look of confusion.

The woman cocked her head and squinted. "Are you lost?" she said in English.

"Oh, my God," Amanda said. She clapped her hands and doubled over in laughter.

Marion glared at her and turned to the woman. "Yes, I'm afraid we've wandered away from the souvenir market and can't find our way back to the ship. Could you help us please?"

"Carlos," the woman called into the house. A barefoot teenager appeared at the door. "Walk these ladies back to their ship. They've gotten all turned around."

"We'll be glad to pay you for your service," Marion said.

"Carlos will not take a peso from you. You are guests in our country. It is our honor to assist you." With that, she turned and went back into the house.

"Oh, thank you so much," Marion said.

They followed Carlos down a series of streets until the ship came into view.

"*Muchas gracias*," Amanda said. Her accent was abysmal, but at least she tried.

"You're very welcome," Carlos said with a smile. "Have a safe trip." He waved goodbye and walked in the direction from which they'd come.

A khaki-uniformed staff person stood, clipboard in hand, foot tapping nervously as they scuttled up the metal ramp that led from the port to the ship. He checked their photo IDs and crossed their names off the roster.

"You were close to becoming residents of Ensenada," he joked—at least Marion *hoped* it was a joke.

"Sorry. Sorry," both women said. Embarrassment flushed their cheeks.

They hustled back to their staterooms. "That about did me in," Amanda said. "I need a nap. Wake me in an hour?"

"Okay. I could use some downtime to read through the activities listed on the schedule," Marion said.

She took the long sheet of paper up to the deck and settled into a lounge chair. The engines made a low hum as the ship eased away from the port. Marion looked up to see seagulls overhead and a pelican lumbering its way through the sky.

She looked back down at the list of activities. Her hand rested just under Restorative Yoga scheduled an hour before dinner on Deck 2. She grinned.

Marion returned to the stateroom with time to spare and decided on a short power nap. She woke with a start.

"Amanda," she said. "Wake up!" Marion sat on the edge of her bed looking anxious.

Amanda grumbled, turned over, and opened her eyes. "What's wrong? Did we miss dinner?"

"No . . . I had a dream."

"Oh no, one of *those* dreams?" Amanda groaned and sat upright facing Marion. Marion tended to 'dream' the future, or 'dream' events from the distant past in detail.

"I'm not sure. It felt portentous. There was a mermaid, who looked a lot like Jeri Kay. She flopped on the deck of this ship. We looked at each other, and I knew she couldn't continue living on land. I didn't help her; I just let her suffer. Finally, she found a way to flop herself overboard." Marion stopped to take a long, deep breath. "I feel horrible. I just stood there. It was as though I was allowing her to die. I could have stopped time and helped her."

One of Marion's psychic gifts was the ability to stop time, which allowed her to absorb details about a situation or even change a potential outcome. As a child at the County Fair, her younger cousin had lost hold of a balloon. The little girl threw a fit as the balloon sailed above the child's head. Although she had no idea how she did it, Marion froze time.

Her uncle grabbed the string and retrieved the balloon that had paused in midair. No one understood exactly what had happened. Her uncle merely said, "Huh," as he tied the end of the string to his daughter's hand.

"At least we know this wasn't a portent of things to come," Amanda said. "Jeri is locked away somewhere for the rest of her life."

"You're probably right," Marion said. "It was just a bad dream." The unease that had filled her ebbed slightly. "Time to change our clothes. Yoga starts in ten minutes."

"Yoga? *Really*? I thought we were on vacation."

Chapter Twenty

"Who knew so many old folks were into yoga," Amanda whispered from her mat next to Marion.

"Maybe it was the word 'restorative' that got to them," Marion mused as she looked around the full room.

Their instructor, Dawn, a tall, lithe woman with long dark-brown hair and walnut-colored eyes entered the room. She pushed the "Play" button on her CD player and relaxing meditation music wafted through the speakers.

A profound calm settled through Marion's body. She peeked at Amanda, who seemed to be experiencing the same sensation.

As the instructor led them through a guided meditation, Marion eased herself from her worries. Dawn's soothing voice held a light French accent, which Marion found charming.

As the woman led the class through a series of yoga poses, Marion leaned near Amanda and whispered, "Is there something familiar about the instructor? Or is it just me?"

During a sideways stretch, Amanda focused on the instructor. There was a familiarity about the face, but the hair, eyes, and voice didn't register. She was slight of build, and the looseness of skin on her arms and legs suggested weight loss. *The cheekbones.*

Something about the cheekbones drew Amanda's attention.

They shifted poses. The instructor was now in profile.

Dawn turned her head toward her students and made eye contact with Amanda. *She looks familiar. Who does she remind me of?* She narrowed her eyes. *No way. She couldn't be here. Could she?*

"*Oh!*" Amanda gasped, pointed at the instructor, and then grabbed her heart. She fell to the floor and, in a puddle of confusion, sat as if stunned.

Marion dropped to her knees next to Amanda and took her hand. "Someone, call a doctor, please," Marion shouted. The oldsters who had been lost in their own meditative reverie sprung out of their poses and gathered around Amanda.

"I'm a retired nurse," one woman said. "Let me check her." She laid Amanda down on the mat. "Can you breathe, honey? Can you hear me?"

Amanda nodded.

The nurse checked Amanda's pulse, her pupils, her breathing. Amanda was pale but not exhibiting symptoms of too much concern. "Are you in pain?" the nurse asked.

Amanda shook her head and reached again for Marion. "The instructor—it's Jeri," she said between ragged breaths. "I don't know how, but it is. I'm sure of it. Wig, contacts, fake accent . . ."

Marion raised her head and searched the room. People parted as the ship's physician made his way to

Amanda's side. The instructor was nowhere to be seen.

The doctor exchanged information with the nurse, checked Amanda's heart, and asked Amanda if she could sit up. With assistance, Amanda struggled to a sitting position. She wildly scanned the room and said, "She's gone." She threw her hands up in despair.

Catching the look in the doctor's eyes, knowing a mental health screening was on its way, she reached for Marion's hand and was pulled to her feet. Both women bolted for the door.

Amanda and Marion stood for a moment outside the yoga room and decided what to do next. They looked both ways down the long corridor of Level 2. "She could be anywhere," Amanda said.

"Let's take a moment and regroup," Marion suggested. She took Amanda by the arm and led her toward a row of deck chairs.

"We don't know for sure that it was Jeri Kay," Marion said reasonably, settling into a chair. "In fact, it *couldn't* be her. She's incarcerated. Perhaps something about her *reminded* you of Jeri."

Amanda shook her head slowly. "No. It was her. I don't know how, but she's here on this ship."

"Perhaps we should tell the staff, or the captain, or someone . . ." Marion was at a loss for further words.

"Uh huh. Tell them there's an escaped psychopath, disguised as a yoga instructor, who kills seniors. Who's going to sound crazy?"

"Oh, yeah. *Déjà vu*." Marion thought back to a crime she'd witnessed *psychically* a few years ago. There was no evidence in the here and now—resulting in a humiliating trip to the psych ward. It took a long time for her restore to restore her credibility.

"Don't you think," Marion suggested, "if Jeri Kay somehow escaped, Detective Bright would let us know? I mean, isn't there some sort of 'duty to warn' or something? You, of all people, would surely be on her personal hit list."

Amanda shuddered. "Our cells are turned off, buried deep in our suitcases. Remember? This was a no-cell vacation—especially with the roaming charges for international calls aboard ship."

Marion looked at Amanda with narrowed eyes and said, "I think it might be worth a few extra dollars to see if our lives are in peril, don't you?"

They scanned the hallways, nooks, and crannies as they hustled toward their stateroom. As soon as they burst into their room, Marion headed directly for the closet.

"Oh, look at this," Amanda mused. She sat down on the edge of her bed. "Fresh towels folded in the shape of a dolphin. Or is that a whale?"

"Amanda, focus," Marion barked as she dug out her cell phone, clicked it on, and waited for the interminable connection signal to light the screen.

Amanda followed suit.

Both phones flashed 'message waiting' icons. Both messages identically imperative: "This is Detective Bright. Call me as soon as you get this message."

"This came in two weeks ago—before we even left," Marion said. "How could we have missed it?"

"Remember, we agreed to turn off our phones after they apprehended Jeri. I guess we forgot to turn them back on," Amanda said. "No one ever calls me, except maybe you from the grocery store."

They exchanged a look of confusion.

"We should call," Marion said.

Amanda pushed the callback number on her screen. The phone rang several times then went to voicemail.

"Detective Bright, this is Amanda Pritchard. We're on a cruise in the Pacific Ocean somewhere on my way back from Mexico." She looked at Marion who made a hurry-up hand gesture.

"We just got your messages, and although you didn't give us much to work with, I'm thinking this is about Jeri Kay."

Marion nodded and mouthed, "Go on."

"Well, the thing is, I'm pretty sure she's onboard with us. I don't know how that could be. . . I mean it's weird, don't you think?"

Marion gritted her teeth with impatience.

"She apparently hired on as a yoga teacher. We spotted her in class—I'm sure she wasn't expecting to see us. She looks entirely different—long dark hair, brown eyes, thinner—but I *know* it was her. She got away when I almost fainted from the shock."

Marion motioned for Amanda to give her the phone.

"Hello, Detective. This is Marion. Please call us back or have the Coast Guard or someone help us. We know it's her . . ." The call disconnected. Marion stared helplessly into the phone and began to shake it to no avail.

Amanda took the phone back, pressed "redial," and heard a busy signal.

"Surely, he'll call back as soon as he gets our message," Marion said. "We'll keep both our phones on and with us at all times. We can try again after dinner."

"Maybe we should order room service," Amanda suggested. "I feel like a sitting duck outside this room. Jeri could jump out anywhere and—"

"And do what?" Marion's voice was stern. "We're onboard a ship. She can't kill us, for God's sake."

Amanda sighed.

"She's the one who ran from us, remember." Marion gestured toward the door.

Unconvinced, Amanda's head turned from side to side, scanning the walkway as they headed to the dining hall.

After a lovely dinner that both women were too anxious to enjoy, they decided to walk the decks and keep an eye out for Jeri. They started on the top deck and worked their way down.

On the middle deck, they paused long enough to take in the stunning sunset.

"Just look at those colors," Marion said. "They remind me of alcohol inks, they're so vivid."

"This is more exercise than I've had in months," Amanda said as she dropped into a deckchair.

"Don't get too comfortable," Marion said. "We have one more deck to go."

"Why are we doing this? She's probably holed up in her stateroom. Why would she be out in public where she could be seen?"

"Oh, *now* you're being reasonable. Out of a thousand-or-so people, we're the only ones who would recognize her," Marion offered. "And what are *we* going to do? She's a tiger, and we're helpless mice." She banged her hand on the railing in frustration.

Moonlight glittered on the ocean surface as Marion and Amanda worked their way to the lower deck. They stood at the rail and looked up at the night sky. In the distance, a passing ship's horn blew a deep and resonant sound. The women shot each other a look that said déjà vu.

Many years ago, Amanda and her lover had been at a sea wall, looking out at a cruise ship in the distance. They listened to the eerie wail of the ship's horn. Suddenly, the passing boat exploded. In her panic, Amanda lost sight of her lover who apparently jumped over the wall into the ocean and swam away, never to be seen again.

"Coincidence," Marion said. "Don't read into it."

Amanda turned away from the railing and noticed a woman farther down the deck walking in their direction. The darkness obscured her facial features. She wore a green body suit that shimmered in the moonlight like wet scales of a fish. Her long hair blew gently in the breeze.

"Oh, my . . . she looks like a mer—" Marion began, then slapped her hand over her mouth. "The dream," she muttered behind her fingers.

The woman stopped short, and then took a step back.

"*Jeri!*" Amanda shouted and bolted toward her.

"Amanda, wait," Marion called out.

Too late. The woman spun around and ran straight to the railing.

"*No!*" Amanda screamed as the woman hurled herself over the railing into the dark sea. There was an almost indiscernible splash twenty feet below.

Marion and Amanda rushed to the railing and peered over the edge. The small lifeboats attached to the ship were on either side of a long stretch of empty space. There was nothing to break the woman's fall.

"Oh, my God," Marion said, gripping the rail. "She can't have survived that!"

Amanda stood, pale and shaking. "Like the mermaid, she couldn't survive living on land either," she said quietly to the black water. "Oh, Jeri." Tears streamed down her face.

Marion pulled her into a tight embrace and let her sob.

"Come on," Marion said when Amanda's tears subsided. "Let's go report this."

They sat crowded in the small security office with two officers and the captain of the ship.

"Someone else is steering the ship, right? Is anyone looking for Jer—Dawn?" Amanda asked the captain. She bounced her knee nervously.

"We've got that covered," the captain said. He smiled and leaned back in his chair.

"So, let me recap what you told our CSO," another security officer said. "The woman you knew as Jeri Kay, who we hired as a yoga teacher under another name, is an alleged serial killer back in California?"

Both women nodded.

"And, to the best of your knowledge, she remanded into custody three weeks before you boarded our ship."

Again, they gave a confirming nod.

"You say you recognized her in the Restorative Yoga class?" He aimed his question at Amanda, "And as a result, you fainted from the shock?"

"I didn't actually faint," Amanda said. Her cheeks tinged pink. "My legs just sort of went out from under me. Everyone crowded around me, and I lost sight of her."

"We looked . . ." Marion added.

"Was there a reason you hesitated to report this directly to security?"

"We didn't think you'd believe us," Marion said with her eyes downcast. "We did try to reach Detective Bright back home though. He was our contact person for this whole, awful ordeal."

"But we weren't able to get through," Amanda added. "Now that Jeri's gone overboard, we knew we had to report it."

"We'll need the contact information for Detective Bright," the captain said.

"Backing up," the officer said, "You saw this woman you believed to be Jeri Kay walking toward you on the lower deck. You called her name, and she ran to the railing and threw herself overboard?" Disbelief tinged his voice.

"Some people just can't live on land," Amanda said cryptically.

The officer raised his eyebrows. "Well," he said, giving his head a little shake. "We are doing a search for our employee, Dawn Rising, and it's true we have not yet been able to locate her. It's a big ship," he added.

"Until we can confirm her absence, or until the Coast Guard finds her, I'm asking that you confine yourself to your stateroom for the duration of the trip," the captain said.

Amanda opened her mouth to protest.

"For your own safety," he added. "We'll provide you with room service at no additional cost."

"Thank you," Marion said. "We'll be happy to comply."

Back in their stateroom, Amanda sat slumped on the edge of her bed. "Why is it that all the women in my life throw themselves into the ocean to avoid me?"

"I don't know that they're necessarily avoiding you. Maybe they're avoiding their own lives," Marion suggested.

"Then why are all the women in my life unable to deal with their own lives?"

"Oh, dear. We could talk about choice, but this probably isn't the time. Let's see what's on the room service menu."

They were a few hours from docking in Long Beach. They scanned the menu and ordered breakfasts from room service.

"Not bad," Amanda commented, lifting the lids on scrambled eggs, bacon, croissants, and a side bowl of fresh fruit. "Although I was looking forward to the buffet in the dining hall."

"By nine o'clock, we'll be off 'house arrest,'" Marion said.

"Not a moment too soon." Amanda threw the last of her belongings into her suitcase. "I'm starting to feel claustrophobic." She settled at the tiny table between their beds.

Both women had checked their phones every few hours, hoping to be within range so they could speak with Detective Bright.

A jarring sound, like a macaw, screeched from Amanda's cell phone. It was her voice mail notification. At about the same time, a discrete buzz emitted from Marion's cell. Both women grabbed their phones and checked their voice mail.

Amanda's mouth made a tight little "O" as she listened to the message. Her eyes blinked compulsively, and her body hunched in tension.

Marion nodded as she listened; her face fixed in a grimace.

While Jeri Kay waited for an evaluation under guard at a psychiatric facility, she had escaped. "Unusual, but not unheard of," the head of the hospital had said apologetically when interviewed. "The guard was found unconscious in Ms. Kay's room with a gash in the back of his head and his gun missing."

A thorough search had turned up nothing. Detective Bright alerted them to be on the lookout. "She might try to contact you," the detective had said. Jeri Kay should be regarded as extremely dangerous.

They both hung up and looked at one another.

"Escaped?" they said in unison.

"The day after she was captured?" Marion looked at the dates stamp on the call and shook her head in amazement. "She must have caught a flight straight to Long Beach."

"She couldn't have known we were going on that cruise ship . . . she just couldn't have," Amanda said, paranoia batting moth wings in her chest.

"She may have had a change of identity, the wig, papers, or whatever was set up in advance, maybe even in preparation of moving to Canada with you," Marion said.

The croissant Amanda holding dropped into her lap. The shaking of her hand moved up her arm, to her shoulders. Her whole body trembled.

Marion set her coffee cup down and reached for Amanda. "What is it? Are you okay?" she said. She took Amanda's hand.

"I have this horrible, weird feeling that Jeri is alive, that she survived the fall, and will surface back in my life . . . when I'm least prepared to deal with it." Amanda's voice cracked with fear. "How will I ever feel safe again?"

Marion squeezed around the table, threw an arm around Amanda's shoulder, and held her tight. "Honey, she couldn't have survived that fall. Eventually, the Coast Guard will find her body, and we can finally put this behind us."

Amanda, unappeased, continued her fretful rant. "What if she had this gig lined up a long time ago. Maybe she never meant to move to Canada with me. Maybe she was going to 'dispose' of me, then head out to sea to start a new life in Mexico."

Marion grabbed Amanda by the shoulders and turned her face-to-face. She shook her head a couple of times, raised her voice, and said, "You've got to stop doing this to yourself. You're just making it worse. Stop it! Please."

Amanda blinked hard and her eyes brimmed with tears. "You've never yelled at me before," she said.

Marion dropped her hands and sat, bewildered, across from Amanda as their breakfast turned cold.

Chapter Twenty-One

"I don't think I want to travel anywhere for a long, long time," Amanda said as she emptied out her suitcase.

Having already unpacked, Marion now sat on the end of Amanda's bed.

"Both times we've traveled together have been pretty disastrous, it's true," Marion said, remembering the Hawaii trip. "I suppose if we ever do get the bug to travel, we could go to one of those travelogue film nights at the university."

"What time was our appointment with Detective Bright?" Amanda asked.

"He said to call when we got settled in. I don't know what more we can tell him, or he us," Marion said. "Jeri Kay will be a missing person until her body is found."

"I just know I'm going to have nightmares about her resurfacing somewhere," Amanda said as she tossed her pantsuit into the laundry basket.

"Remember, don't wash that with dark clothes," Marion said.

Amanda turned her head and fixed Marion with a stare. "Were you one of those bossy wives?"

Marion opened her mouth as if to defend herself, then closed it again. She took a breath and exhaled slowly.

"Yes, I suppose I was. Sometimes I hear my mother's voice come out of my mouth."

Amanda tossed her suitcase in the closet and plunked herself down on her bed next to Marion.

"You ever think of getting remarried?"

"Never," Marion responded without hesitation.

"Good," Amanda said, grinning. "Because I don't know what I'd do without you."

The two women sat with the truth of that between them like a physical presence.

"Too bad you're not gay," Amanda said. They'd never wandered into this territory.

"Well, I'm not," Marion said. Her tone was brusquer than needed.

"S'okay by me," Amanda said. "You're not my type, anyway."

"Then why did you say that?"

Amanda sat with that a while, then said, "Sometimes I feel lonely."

Marion raised her eyebrows and pulled back ever so slightly.

"Oh, God . . . lonely, *not* horny," Amanda said. "I'm way beyond that. It's just that I feel isolated from people who 'get me' on that level . . . like how I could have fallen for Jeri, or why my heart is broken even though she turned out to be a crazy serial killer. She seemed to get me."

"In what way?"

"It's an outsider kind of thing, I guess."

"You consider yourself an outsider?" Marion asked.

After a moment, both women burst into laughter.

"Seriously," Amanda said after regaining her breath. "There was at least the illusion, for a moment in time, that Jeri 'understood' me, knew who I was." She remembered Jeri's eyes falling on her as she scanned the classroom of students and the feeling of shared intimacy at the coffee house.

"It's that *gaydar* thing, right?" Marion said. "You're right. I don't get that. But I can see how it would feel important to be known on that level. It's an acknowledgment or validation of something shared . . . like in the hetero world, the way some women are around a pregnant woman."

"Thank you," Amanda said, her eyes moist with appreciation.

The remainder of the day was spent catching up on laundry, grocery shopping, errand running, and falling back into their routine. A Netflix binge filled their evening.

"Why do you like those programs about dysfunctional families?" Marion asked as Amanda clicked off the TV. "Everyone is always in everyone else's business, talking over one another, lying, cheating."

"Hey, at least they interact," Amanda said, to which Marion could say nothing.

"As interesting as it was to sleep on a ship, I'm looking forward to a bed that doesn't rock," Amanda said as she gathered up her belongings and headed toward her room.

She glanced back over her shoulder. "Aren't you going to bed?"

"I'm feeling a little restless. Maybe I'll try some warm milk. Sleep well," Marion called.

As the milk heated on the stove, Marion padded to the back, then the front door, making sure the locks were secure. She hadn't wanted to add to Amanda's paranoia, but she had an uncomfortable feeling that they had not seen the last of Jeri Kay. How that was even possible, she had no idea.

When she did finally turn in for the night, her sleep was fitful. Dark, waterlogged, seaweed-strewn images played in the subconscious of her mind. A bloated corpse floated up onto shore, arose, shook the sand from itself, and wandered along the coast.

The next image was a zombie-like visage of Jeri Kay. She stood over a sleeping Amanda, knife posed, and ready to strike. Marion awoke, screaming and thrashing beneath her covers.

Amanda rushed in to find Marion, one foot on the floor, the other caught up in her sheet, looking terrified.

"It's okay. We're safe. It was only a bad dream," Amanda said. She sat down next to Marion, took her icy-cold hand, and rubbed it briskly. "It was a Jeri Kay thing, wasn't it?"

Marion nodded. She took several deep breaths.

"Can you tell me about it?" Amanda said as she helped Marion back under the covers and tucked them under her chin.

Marion sorted quickly among her options. "No," she decided. "I can't remember," she lied.

"Do you want me to leave both our bedroom doors open for the rest of the night?" Amanda asked.

"Yes. Thank you. I think I'd feel safer."

"Okay. See you in the morning," Amanda said.

The following day, they sat across from Detective Bright in his downtown office.

"You have the whole story, as best as we know it," Amanda said. "Do you have any updates for us?"

"I'm afraid not. Unless the Coast Guard finds her . . ."

"Remains?" Amanda suggested. She had a vivid enough imagination to guess what might be left of a body retrieved after a week in the ocean.

"Yes," the detective replied. "If she survived the fall and found her way to land, she is listed as a wanted person, armed and dangerous. We've notified the FBI and local officials up and down the coast and in Mexico. She wouldn't get far."

"You don't know Jeri Kay," Marion said. "I feel terrible hoping she's dead, but . . ."

"Understandable," Detective Bright said.

They shook hands and left his office.

Once outside, Amanda said, "I'll drop you off at home. I have some stuff to take care of. That okay?"

"Sure. I noticed the leaves didn't stop falling in the backyard just because we were on vacation," Marion said. "I have plenty to do today,"

As Marion got out of the car, she said, "Have fun."

It was met with a grimace that was perhaps an attempt at a smile.

Hmm, that was weird, Marion thought.

As her source had instructed, Amanda drove past the outskirts of town and turned onto a rough, unmarked road. Ahead lie the remains of an abandoned basket factory. It was mostly rubble now, tagged with graffiti, strewn with broken bottles and debris.

She drove to the back of the property where an old tool shed tilted on its foundation. After parking the car, she rolled down the window and listened to the stillness. Her knuckles were white as she gripped the steering wheel.

Within moments, the metal door of the shed creaked on its hinges and opened enough for a stocky-built man with a black nylon over his face to stick his head out.

Amanda got out of the car, leaned against the fender, and crossed an ankle over the other, casual-like. She couldn't remember what had prompted her to put her life at risk like this. She could be robbed, shot, and left to die out here in this unforsaken place. God—no one knew where she was.

The man, dressed from head to toe in black, pushed the door open and stepped through.

Amanda could feel the corners of her mouth twitch. *This is like being stuck in a terrible B movie,* she thought. The comic relief helped her take a deep breath and step forward.

"You have the money?" the man said. His voice distorted behind the stocking.

"You have the gun?" she said. "Show me."

From his jacket pocket, he pulled out the .38 revolver and held it, barrel down, in front of him.

"I assume it's stolen," Amanda said. "Has the serial number been filed off?"

"Untraceable," the man mumbled.

"Is it—?"

"Look, you want it or not?" The man fidgeted, rocking back and forth on his feet.

Not someone you want feeling anxious, Amanda thought. Yes," Amanda said.

Her 'source,' from her old days working with people on both sides of the law, had provided her with this reference. She hoped the adage, *honor among thieves*, held true as she withdrew a wad of cash from her pocket and stepped forward.

The man, having re-pocketed the gun, grabbed and counted the money. Sweat broke out on Amanda's forehead.

Apparently satisfied, the man handed her the gun.

"Bullets?" she said.

"Loaded," he replied. "Do you even know how to shoot that thing?" His voice dripped sarcasm.

Amanda snorted, grabbed the gun, and forced herself to walk calmly back to her car. Her hand shook as she opened the car door.

She checked to make sure the safety was on then crammed the gun into her pocket, climbed into the car, and drove back down the rut-filled road. Sweat drenched her back, and she shivered involuntarily.

Just another day-in-the-life, she told herself. Nothing to get upset about. Guilt niggled at the edges of her consciousness. She knew Marion disapproved of guns, especially in the home. *Well*, she reasoned, *that's why I didn't tell her*.

She patted her pocket and felt a sense of calm settle over her body. By the time she reached home, she felt almost giddy having reclaimed some sense of control over the situation. The giddiness wavered momentarily when she considered whether she could actually shoot Jeri if it came to that.

Yes, she decided. *When it comes down to her or me, I win*. She nodded, satisfied.

Marion was still out back raking leaves. Amanda slipped into her bedroom, looked back over her shoulder, and quickly stuck the gun at the far back of her bedside table drawer. For good measure, she covered it with a colorful brochure with instructions on what to do if you think you're having a heart attack.

Marion would never go through my things. Amanda exhaled slowly.

"You're back," Marion said.

Amanda jumped, slapped her hand over her heart, and chuckled.

"What's so funny?" Marion asked.

"Too hard to explain," Amanda said, as she nudged the drawer closed with her hip.

Chapter Twenty-Two

Late autumn flirted with winter. The days were warm and sunny, the nights chilly and damp. More often than not, dew dripped from the trees to the ground in the morning, which signaled the approach of the rainy season.

"What shall we do next?" Marion said, thumbing through the Autumn-Winter Activity Guide. She hoped to reestablish some semblance of routine in their lives.

They sat under an oak tree in their immaculately leafless backyard for a midday tea break. A leaf dared to tumble from an overhanging branch and land with a *thip* near Marion's chair. She reached over, grabbed it, and set it on the table between them.

"You know, it's okay to have leaves on the ground. It's sort of nature's way of indicating the change of seasons," Amanda said.

"I've had enough change for a while," Marion replied. "You're avoiding my question. What shall we do next?"

"Do we really have to *do* something? Can't we perhaps just *be* in our retirement?" Amanda groused.

"I don't want to be one of those old ladies who wind up in a care facility because she stopped using her mind, and it went all soggy." Marion turned the page loudly. "Oh, here . . ." she said. "How about a Wine Appreciation class?"

"I appreciate wine quite enough, thank you." "Here's one on how to make your own soap using goat milk."

"I can see that leading to 'How to Raise your own Goats.' No, I don't think so."

Marion raised her eyebrows. "Goats eat grass, right? That could be useful," she said, glancing around the yard. She closed the guide with a resigned sigh. "The symphony? A little culture couldn't hurt us." She turned a beseeching look toward Amanda.

Amanda threw up her hands. "Oh, for God sake. The symphony, if we must. What could possibly go wrong at a symphony? Order the season tickets. I'll go dust off my top hat—with our luck, the diva soprano will look remarkably like Jeri Kay." With that, Amanda grabbed her mug of tea and went inside.

Marion rolled her eyes.

Later, in her room, Amanda pulled her journal from under her pillow. She'd heard on *Oprah* that journaling was an excellent way to dispel some of the emotional garbage that she'd otherwise carry around in her psyche.

How is it possible for two such different women to share a home and a life? Is that what we're doing? Sharing a life?

Amanda leaned back on her pillow and pondered that thought until her eyes closed, and the pen slipped from her hand.

The next day, while Amanda was gadding about, doing whatever it was Amanda did when Marion had nothing planned, Marion rummaged through the medicine cabinet in the bathroom.

"Advil. I know we have some somewhere," she mumbled. As she moved bottles and containers about, she checked the expiration dates. "Does Mentholatum ever go bad?" she mused aloud. She tossed a bottle of eye drops and an expired box of allergy medication into the trash.

Her shoulders and back had stiffened up from the exertion of yesterday's leaf raking. *Advil. I need Advil. Where on earth would it be, if not here?*

"Ah," she said, remembering the tube of Arnica Gel in Amanda's bedside table. Good for the bumps and bruises she sprouted moving through the world in her less-than-graceful manner. *Perhaps Amanda had squirreled away the Advil as well.*

It was an unspoken agreement that they respected each other's privacy, always knocked on closed doors before entering. *Surely, Amanda wouldn't mind if I checked her room. She wouldn't want me to wait in pain, for heaven knows how long until she got home.*

Out of habit, she tapped on the closed bedroom door then entered. She pulled open the drawer to the nightstand and rummaged around. No Advil. She searched again, this time uncovering . . .

A gun!

Marion withdrew her hand as if she had encountered a rattlesnake, coiled and ready to strike. She stared at the dull metal.

What was Amanda doing with a gun? They'd talked about that. No weapons in the house, the exception being the baseball bat Amanda kept in her bedroom closet.

This was unacceptable. She would have a talk with Amanda later. Until then, Marion very carefully removed the gun. She carried it into her own room and put it high up on her closet shelf safely out of Amanda's reach. *With as jumpy as Amanda has been lately, we just can't afford any accidents.*

Advil forgotten, she booted up her computer and did a search for symphony tickets. To her delight, there was a concert that evening, something by a new composer, an experimental piece, whatever that meant. She ordered balcony tickets to give them a birds-eye view for their first concert and checked that task off her list.

Time for the task she was least looking forward to. She pulled her bag of alcohol inks and accouterments out from under the bed and did an assessment of their value.

With her computer still on, she clicked on Craig's List, and with some regret, placed a 'for sale' ad. The association with this art form—dead old women, serial killers—was just too much for her psyche to handle. Out of sight, permanently, out of mind, hopefully.

Check.

Back to her never-ending to-do list.

Around five o'clock, Amanda returned.

"You've been gone forever," Marion said with a smile. "Have a good afternoon?"

"Yes, I did. I ran into an old friend at the coffee shop. Got a chance to catch up. Reminded me of back in the day, when I was more social," she said, her voice wistful.

"Oh," Marion said with a start. "That reminds me, we have symphony tickets for tonight." She checked her watch. "There's just enough time for a quick dinner and a change of clothes."

"Thank you," she said after a moment. "That's something I wouldn't have thought to do. Although, I might have chosen baseball tickets."

Marion shook her head. "Your welcome."

"Okay, that wasn't so bad," Amanda said as they followed the throng out of the symphony hall and headed for their car. "Although I'm not sure I understood the music."

"Not so bad?" Marion said, aghast. "It was incredible. Marvelous. How do they even know how to do that—all those instruments working in perfect sync with one another?"

"Well, there's the music . . . and the conductor."

"You know what I mean. It's talent, honed to its finest expression. I feel rapturous," Marion said as she buckled her seatbelt.

While Marion floated on the music in her head, across town, a shadow slid into their backyard and nestled behind the oak tree like an extra layer of bark.

The house was stuffy from the day's warmth when they returned. Both women busied themselves opening windows, latching screen doors, turning on fans.

Amanda settled down in the living room and turned on the TV. She scanned the programs, found nothing to her liking, and walked into the kitchen to make a bedtime snack.

"Apparently I've had all the stimulation I can handle for one evening," she said to Marion who was emptying the dishwasher. "Think I'll turn in early. Will you close up the house?"

"Sure," Marion said. She raised her eyebrows. "Are you really eating leftover pizza before bed?"

Amanda gave her an impish grin. "Yes, I am, Mom." She swaggered out of the kitchen.

Marion tsked. "Oh . . ." she said, remembering she wanted to talk with Amanda about the gun. Sensing it might be a touchy subject just before bedtime, she decided to leave it for the morning.

Marion curled up in the side chair, thumbed through the symphony program, and reviewed the list of musicians. She thought she'd recognized a former coworker from the copy shop on stage, but no names looked familiar.

With a yawn, she tossed the program in the wastebasket and set about closing the doors and windows for the night. The light was still on in Amanda's room. Marion sighed at the thought of her roommate eating pizza at this hour of the night. *Oh, well, what can you do?*

Braced by pillows, Amanda sat against her headboard, writing in her journal. She consumed the rest of a cold pizza straight from the box.

She put down the pen, closed the journal, and slipped it into her bedside table drawer. She patted the drawer, feeling safe and secure from her recent purchase.

Before crawling into bed, she lowered her window, allowing the fresh evening air to come through a two-inch gap. She promised herself that next summer she would put a screen on that window.

Amanda turned off the light and snuggled down under the covers. She smiled at the slice of moonlight coming through the window. *Nature's nightlight*, she remembered telling herself somewhere back in childhood. Within moments, she was asleep.

The moon had shifted, and the room was pitch black when Amanda woke to a scraping sound. She sensed movement at her window. She quickly turned to her bedside table drawer, yanked it open, and jammed her hand to the back.

No gun!

Instinct overtook reason, and she screamed as the window was pulled open. She threw herself on the floor and rolled under her bed.

Down the hall, Marion bolted upright in bed. She jumped up, ran to the closet, grabbed the gun, and raced to Amanda's room.

As she burst through the door, she clicked on the overhead light, illuminating the bizarre tableau of a woman standing at the side of Amanda's bed, hand raised overhead, wielding a long dagger.

Jeri Kay turned her evil glare to Marion, who used that moment to unlatch the safety on the gun, point, and shoot.

Time froze.

A ghastly grimace rearranged Jeri Kay's face as she fell to the floor with a sickening thud, inches from where Amanda lay under the bed. Blood spilled from a gaping hole in her neck.

Marion dropped the gun to the floor and stood, stunned, shaking, and unable to think.

"Help, help," Amanda gasped as she rolled away from the body.

Marion forced her wobbly legs to move to the other side of the bed. She reached down and helped pull Amanda out.

They clung to each other, afraid to let go, afraid to deal with whatever would come next.

"I killed her. I killed her," Marion mumbled into Amanda's neck.

"Shhh," Amanda whispered as she patted Marion on the back. "It's going to be okay." They rocked back and forth comforting one another. "You saved my life," Amanda said.

Moments later, when they'd each caught their breath, they moved apart but clutched hands as they worked their way back around the bed.

"It's her, isn't it?" Amanda said.

Marion nodded.

A chilly breeze drifted through the open window and rippled the curtains.

"No, I mean it's *her*, the Jeri we knew," Amanda clarified.

"Oh, my God!" Marion gasped. "If this is Jeri Kay, who was the woman who jumped off the ship?" They stared at each other, stupefied.

"I really hate to say this, but you know what we have to do next," Amanda said. They backed out of the room.

Marion ducked into her bedroom, grabbed her cell phone, and brought it to the couch where they huddled together. "Do we have the death penalty here in California?" she asked as she dialed 9-1-1.

"I'm not sure," Amanda muttered. "I'll put on the coffee pot. It's going to be a long night." She glanced at the clock. "Make that morning."

Amanda and Marion had just finished rehashing the last hour. Two federal agents, the police Sargent, two officers, and Detective Bright sat crammed in the small living room. They sipped their coffee as the story unfolded. The Coroner came and went. Both women shuddered as Jeri's draped body was removed from the back bedroom.

"Well, one mystery solved," the detective said. "At least we know it wasn't Jeri Kay who was aboard the ship. Most probably she's been hiding out around here all along."

"Hard to imagine," said one of the officers. "With the manpower we've had looking for her."

"Until we had a break in this case, we were keeping some information quiet regarding the other woman, who by the way, was found by the Coast Guard not far off the California coast," one of the agents said.

"Alive?" Amanda said, leaning forward. Her hand shook so hard, coffee splashed onto the table as she set her cup down.

"No," the other federal agent said. "The woman the cruise line hired as a yoga teacher was Dawn Rising, transgender male-to-female. Her former name was Gerald Kalzinski, Gerry for short."

"The resemblance to Jeri was uncanny," Amanda said.

"It seems," the first agent took up the story, "that Mr. Kalzinski had some trouble with the Jersey mob, back in the day. He was on their hit list. Apparently, Dawn was looking forward to leaving her old identity behind and starting a new and untraceable life south of the border."

"So, when Amanda yelled, 'Jeri,' on deck," Marion ventured, "the poor woman thought Amanda was part of the mob. She'd been found. So, she panicked and threw herself overboard?" She put her hand over her heart. "Oh, how tragic is that?"

"That's what we surmised happened," the agent said.

"I feel terrible," Amanda said, shaking her head.

"Oh, honey, it's not your fault." Marion patted Amanda's hand.

"Getting back to the matter at hand," the sergeant said. "What *does* appear to be your fault." He eyed Marion. "Is the death of Jeri Kay."

Marion shrunk back into the couch and stared at her hands, clasped tightly in her lap.

Amanda jumped to her feet. "But, she was protecting me from a murderer," she said. "Surely, that's worth something."

"That will all get sorted out in court," the sergeant said, "but for now . . ." He nodded to one of his men.

The officer rose and said, "Marion Knox, you are under arrest for the murder of Jeri Kay. Please stand."

Marion stood, her face void of emotion, and was handcuffed and read her rights.

"I'll call a lawyer," Amanda said as Marion was led out. "We'll get you bailed out as soon as possible."

Chapter Twenty-Three

Marion, seen as a very low-risk for escape, was bailed out the next morning.

Through a mind-boggling whirlwind of court appearances with her attorney at her side, and Amanda nervously wringing her hands in the galley, the final judgment was voluntary manslaughter, with mitigating circumstances—*many* mitigating circumstances, her attorney was able to argue.

The judge, who appeared to have developed a permanent crease in his forehead by the end of the ordeal, sentenced her to three-years in prison, suspended, and ordered her to serve a one-year probation.

"You realize, Mrs. Knox, this means no fraternizing with felons from here forward. Do you think you can manage that?" The corners of his mouth twitched into something resembling a smile.

"Yes, your Honor, I can certainly do that," she said. She sent a pointed *did-you-hear-that* look to Amanda who sat grinning widely.

"And, no weapons are to be kept in your home," the judge added. This time he sent a smile-deflating look at Amanda.

Later that day, in an attempt to get back to their normal routine, the two women had lunch under the oak tree in the backyard.

"I don't know," Amanda said. "It seems like a year's probation is a little excessive." She took a bite of her sandwich.

"Well, I did kill someone after all." A shudder passed through Marion. She set her sandwich back down on her plate.

"I didn't know you could shoot like that," Amanda said, her voice tinged with awe. "Right through the neck. Wow."

Marion cringed at the memory. "Dumb luck, I guess. I think I closed my eyes. As long as we're on the subject, didn't we have an agreement about weapons in the house?"

Amanda grimaced. "Won't happen again. I just kept having this irrational feeling that Jeri was going to rise from the dead and come kill me."

"Well, you weren't too far off. Nonetheless, I wish you'd told me."

"I wish you'd told me you'd taken my gun," Amanda said.

They sat in silence.

"Guess I'm not very good at this roommate thing," Amanda finally said.

"I have a confession to make," Marion said. "I didn't tell you about the dream I had of Jeri Kay standing over your bed with a knife. Didn't want to worry you."

Amanda's jaw dropped.

"We're a work in progress," Marion said. She reached over and gave Amanda a hug.

Jo Lauer

Other Books by Jo Lauer

Second Floor, Front
(A Little Old Ladies Mystery)

Returning:
A Collection of Stories

An Unlikely Trio

Best Laid Plans

Gone Awry

Jo Lauer

ABOUT THE AUTHOR

Jo Lauer is a psychotherapist by day. Her articles, essays, and stories appear in numerous publications. In addition to her latest novel—the first in the "Little Old Ladies Mystery" series—*Second Floor, Front*, her books include, *Returning: A Collection of Stories*, and a cozy mystery trilogy: *An Unlikely Trio*, *Best Laid Plans*, and *Gone Awry*. She lives with her stuffed raven, Loudly, in Santa Rosa, CA. You can find out more about the author by visiting her website at www.jolauer.com.

She cradled the sides of his head in her hands. His curly reddish-brown hair fell below his ears and his well-trimmed beard suited his handsome face. An urge to kiss him swept over her. As if he read her mind, he lifted her from the chair and brushed a kiss across her lips. She melted into his embrace and rested her head on his chest. His body was hard as molded steel, and his muscles rippled as he enfolded her in a tender embrace. She'd never been this protected and cared for in her thirty years of life.

He put his hand under her chin and lifted her face. His lips were on hers before she could speak. Searching. Probing. Demanding. A man, a woman each lost in the intensity of desire. The image of him naked made her core lust after a connection. She let herself feel for the first time in years, feel the affection, feel the lust, feel the love. When the kiss was over, her body instinctively gravitated toward him desiring more.

"Come." He steadied her with his arm around her waist and guided her to his bedroom. "I want you to rest, comfortable in a bed, not on the floor."

They entered a bright room with a large ornately carved bed, dressing table and mirror, and large wardrobe. The Scotsman appeared to be a strong, rough cowboy, but she was learning he was more refined and intelligent than Walker. How could she compare a devil to Callum MacPhilip?

Previous releases by Jane Lewis

Love at Five Thousand Feet
The Barnstormer
The Lady Flyer
Home In Wylder